SHADOW OF THE MOON

JM MADDEN

ACKNOWLEDGMENTS

I always forget to add people into the acknowledgements, and I apologize for that.

This one is to my beta reader team, because you all kick butt! I love your dedication to my books and making them the best they can be. You all have such different perspectives, which I love. You make the story more full, and I love you all for that!

Dev sighed as he glanced over at the buzzing cellphone. Unknown again. In the days of spam call after spam call, the caller had to assume that he wouldn't pick up. If they left a message, he would return the call, but until then they could rot in hell for all Dev cared.

"No, I don't need to renew my car's warranty," he murmured to no one in particular.

He reached for the yellow wire at the back of the camera he was mounting and paired it with the corresponding wire coming out of the wall. Using a blue butt, he twisted the two wires together and secured the connection. Then he did the same with the blue wire and screwed the device into the pre-drilled holes. Fitting the smoke detector over top of it, he snapped it into place. The camera was secure when he was done, and he knew most people wouldn't even see it when they walked through the main door of the Allen Insurance Company.

Jack Allen was a bit of a drinking buddy, and he'd given Dev this job when he lost a bet as to whether or not Dev could find whoever was responsible for stealing all the creamer from his personal fridge. It was a ridiculous bet, but a genuine concern for Jack, because someone had been in his private office when he wasn't there. Anyway, it got Dev's foot in the door to do security hookups for the entire Allen Insurance Group, which covered most of the lower half of Tennessee state. It was a good gig, a *big* gig, and Jack had signed the contract, shaking his head and chuckling the entire time.

Dev didn't care. It started out as fun, but there'd been a thread of calculation when he'd made the bet. There might have also been a thread of calculation when he picked the bar he knew Jack drank at every Friday. This was a big contract, and he would not let it slip away. When the direct approach hadn't worked on Jack, he'd had to be a little sly. Whatever, it was a long-term contract, and he would do the best security work he could. Might even be enough work to pay for another tech.

Dev had five men on staff, now, working every day to keep up with the contracts. They were all men he trusted and had vetted and trained himself. Two of them he considered true friends.

His phone buzzed again, this time with a text message.

Moon Devil.

Senses suddenly on high alert, he flicked his gaze around, but didn't see anyone or anything suspicious. The windows, though, only showed dark night outside, with a few parking lot mercury vapor lights, their orange glow not enough to chase away the night. There could be an entire SEAL team on the other side of the lot, and he would have no way of knowing.

Moon Devil. Two words that sent chills down his spine. No one had called him that for a very long time, going on three years. Had it really been that long? Yes. He remembered the date his life had gone to hell as if it had been yesterday, because it had sent him into the worst professional crisis he'd ever had. Worst personal crisis, as well. It had ruined him in every way imaginable, and now someone was using his name to get to him.

His throat closed up and he turned his attention away from the phone and windows. Whoever was on the other end of that text message he wanted to avoid, because all the old shit would get stirred up; the betrayal, the loss, the desperation. It had taken him a long time to get back on an even keel, and he wasn't going to risk it for anything. That name was dead to him.

The phone buzzed again, and he looked at it, reluctantly. *Tango 11 is on the loose.*

His determination not to submit wavered, shock rolling through him. Whoever it was, they knew how to get to him. Was it the Navy? CIA? One of his former best friends that had turned on him when his life and reputation had gone to hell?

Jaw firming, he powered down the phone and tossed it into the toolbox. It was after seven at night, so he technically wasn't on the clock anymore. Since he was the boss, he ran his schedule as he liked, preferring to do the wiring of the security after business hours so that the employees had no idea he'd even been there. Because that was who he was after, the employees. When a business got to be as big as Allen Insurance Group, internal theft and embezzlement could be an enormous problem, and since insurance companies were one of the top three companies that experienced employee theft, Dev knew he would find something. Or someone. Even Jack knew something was going on with his bottom line, but he couldn't pinpoint it.

That was why Dev was in here doing all the grunt work

himself. Just like with the damn creamer, he would figure out who it was and let Jack decide how he wanted to deal with it.

Glancing at the toolbox, he almost gritted his teeth, then he breathed through it. Who was it trying to pin him down?

Definitely no one he needed to talk to.

What if 11 was loose, though?

Normally, his nerves were rock solid, but when the phones in the office began to ring in stereo, his anxiety spiked. The front windows were dark. Jack had given him the alarm code to let himself in and do what needed done. There was no one else here, which meant no one should be calling trying to reach someone.

Looking up the number to the insurance company was probably not that hard, but getting every single phone at every single desk in the place to ring at once? When they all had to have separate numbers? That was skill. Or good technicians.

They weren't going to let him avoid them.

Fuck.

The sense of being under surveillance was not comfortable. Normally, he was the one surveilling, so the feeling chafed. He did not want to answer to whoever was jerking his leash.

Did he dare *not* respond?

Reaching into his toolbox, he retrieved his phone and powered it on. Once it went through the startup, it immediately began to ring. He swiped his thumb across the screen and sank down into an office chair. "Hello."

"Hello, Chief Petty Officer Kreed. I'm glad you decided to pick up."

He'd expected a gruff man's voice, something military, but it was the exact opposite. The woman on the other end of the line sounded polished and educated, her voice mellow and a little sardonic.

Dev scowled. "I'm not in the Navy anymore, ma'am, so you can drop the title."

"As you wish, Devlin. My name is Charley, and I'm about to change your life."

Dev snorted and shook his head. "I don't want my life changed, Charley. I'm content doing what I'm doing."

On the other end of the line, Charley sighed. "I thought you might say that, and I'm glad you're doing so well, but I don't know that the world is going to fare as well."

Dev clenched his jaw, hating that this nameless, faceless woman was trying to guilt trip him. "I did my time in the Navy. Someone else can take care of 11. He's the CIA's responsibility."

"Hm, yes, that's what we've been told as well, but he's too dangerous to leave free. We've already gotten reports of missing shipments of components. One of his former compatriots is also missing, and we assume they're together. It's only a matter of time before he wreaks havoc and kills again, we assume around the September 11th anniversary."

Dev rocked back in the chair, anger surging through him. "Why the fuck are you even calling me? 11 is not my issue anymore. The CIA made that very clear when they burned me after I went along with their crazy extraction plan. I'm done. The man can blow Washington off the map for all I care."

He said it off-hand, but Washington probably would be Cole Regent's target. It had been his focus for many years, and he'd been blowing up smaller targets to prepare for his main target, the heart of evil, as he called it, Washington, D.C. Honestly, Dev kind of agreed with the guy, but it wasn't his responsibility anymore.

When Dev's team had gotten the call to escort the home-grown paramilitary extremist from CIA Headquarters to the airport, Devlin had thought little of it. It was just another job. Then two men with CIA badges had approached him. Actually, looking back, he thought it had been the Special Activities Center that had approached him. They were the black ops side of the CIA, doing the especially dirty stuff that the government would disavow if caught. They wanted Devlin to shoot Regent, but they wanted him to 'wound' rather than 'kill', because Regent had information to share on a wider network of international collaborators, the Russians specifically. They wanted it to look like a legitimate kill, though, to throw off those international friends that were watching Regent. The operatives would remove the target from the scene and make it look like the informant had died. Then Regent would be housed in a secret facility while the Agency tapped the info he had. Once he'd been interrogated and the information extracted, then Regent would quietly disappear. Devlin assumed that they would take him out themselves, and clean up the mess when they were done extracting information.

But it sounded like the team had botched the job.

Of course they had.

The two men had presented Dev with a doctored recording of his own voice making a deal with some international conglomeration for half a million dollars to take out Regent, and it was at that point he knew he was fucked no matter what he did. If he cooperated with the CIA extraction story and took the shot, they would dishonorably discharge him. If he *didn't* cooperate, an 'informant' would offer evidence that Amberly was dirty, and she would go to prison for the rest of her life for helping kill Regent for money.

That was the deal breaker. Amberly was his weak point, and he'd known he would go along with whatever they said in order to keep her safe.

The CIA had sworn to him that his sacrifice for the country had been noted, then they'd burned him, reporting that Devlin had gone rogue in some kind of revenge killing. Since the killing worked in their favor, the CIA would not be pursuing charges. That was actually what they'd told his commanding officers, that they'd taken his record into account and that he should *just* be dishonorably discharged.

The shame that had come from that two-month period would follow him for the rest of his life. Over and over again, he'd had to bite his tongue in fury at not being able to lash out at the sneers and jibes, at not being able to defend himself. His supposed friends had all abandoned him. And Amberly... Well, she'd done what she needed to do to protect herself.

"What if I told you I could get you reinstated, retroactively, and your back pay reimbursed to you? All charges would be struck from your record and the discharge would be noted as honorable."

Dev laughed bitterly. "I'd say you're full of shit, just like every other bureaucrat out there. I couldn't care less about the Navy anymore. They have nothing for me. You all can burn in hell for all I care."

"Does that go for Amberly Temple as well? Because she's about to walk into a shit storm, and right this minute you're the only one that can save her."

Amberly Temple... yeah, she was his Kryptonite. And even this long after she'd left him in the cold, he would go to her in a heartbeat if she called. "And why is that," he asked, trying to sound as disinterested as she had.

"Amberly is a big girl, able to make her own decisions about her life. She certainly doesn't want me involved in any part of it."

"That may be true," the woman agreed, "but she's digging into things that could get her killed."

Yes, his gut clenched, but he forced out a laugh. "It is not my job to look after my wife. I gave that up three years ago when she kicked me out of the house."

He hated even responding to the woman on the phone, but his pride demanded it. If Amberly had stood by him, it would have been one thing. But she hadn't even blinked, as she'd told him he needed to get out of the house before she shot him. He'd packed a bag with the bare essentials and walked out, knowing, hoping, that she would be protected if he took the fall.

At least that had been the plan. If Regent was on the loose, obviously the plan had gone to shit. Whoever the two men had been had fucked up. Regent was never supposed to hit the streets again.

"She works for the CIA. I think she'll be fine."

There was a silence on the other end of the line, as if she were waiting for him to catch up. "Why do you think she's in trouble," he asked, in spite of himself.

"Because she's about to stumble onto a very dangerous piece of information that is going to get her killed if she approaches the wrong person with it. She needs backup, and there's no one in her department she trusts. And very few that she should."

Dev knew that feeling well. For the past few years, he'd been on his own, rebuilding a life that didn't revolve around the Navy and killing people. If Amberly was out in the cold...

Fuck me running...

"So, what exactly are you calling me for? To get me to kill 11 or backup Amberly?"

"Why can't it be both," Charley asked, her voice low. "Plus, you'll have an incredible payout in the end."

"I don't care about money," he snapped.

"Then maybe you'll care about reestablishing your good name? You had an incredible record in the SEALs. Your kill count still stands in your team, and people still talk about some of your shots."

Who the hell was this woman? "You're not CIA, or any of the other alphabet soup agencies I'm familiar with. Who are you?"

Charley hummed on the other end of the line. "Let's just say I'm an extremely concerned citizen with a lot of money and friends in prominent places and leave it at that."

Of course, she would not tell him. The higher-ups never did.

"You have 12 hours to get your ass to Chicago, where Amberly has a meeting with an informant. I'll send you location details."

"I haven't even agreed to do this," he said, voice aggravated.

"Yes, you have, Devlin. As soon as Amberly was a part of it, I knew you wouldn't tell me no. Your task is to rescue your ex because she has a general love for her country and always does what's right, and take out 11, for real this time. No botched shots, no CIA interference. I want him gone, before he starts killing again. And you have carte blanche to take out anyone affiliated with him. We'll watch and tamp down response, if necessary."

Dev sighed, wondering what the hell he was thinking, because he knew he was going to do it. "Fine. Do I have any backup at all or is this a one-man op?"

"Well, save your wife and you'll have a team." Her voice was sardonic.

Devlin snorted. "Right... Assuming she just doesn't kill me on sight."

"Regent will head to the upper Midwest, Montana, we assume. His brand of crazy fits pretty well up there. He still has connections to his father's paramilitary group, but he's created his own, as well. They're called The Blade."

"Roger that."

Actually, he had notes at home about the escort job, and the preliminary dossier when Regent was designated a VIP. Dev probably had all the information he needed to find the man, especially if he was bright enough to return home. "How do I contact you?"

"I'll keep this line available, though I can't always answer it."

"Fine."

He hung up then, because there wasn't anything else to say. Glancing around the office, he sighed. Jack was not going to be happy.

2

The hairs on the back of her neck were going to fricking run off if they stood up any harder.

Amberly glanced around her as surreptitiously as she could, without moving her head. She bumped her sunglasses up with a fingertip, and tilted her head back into the breeze. The bustling Chicago streets were an assault on the senses, and she was at peak alertness. The covert informant should have been here ten minutes ago. If he stood her up after she'd traveled all this way...

Maybe this was a power play. They did that sometimes. Reaching forward, she took a sip of her coffee, then nibbled a piece of danish. It was stale, though, and not very appetizing. Maybe when she got out of here, she would treat herself to a real meal.

The chances of this panning out, though, were pretty slim.

Deputy Director Brown would be so happy when she reported back that another cold case was going to stay cold.

Something niggled at her about this one, though. This

was the big botched transport job that had sent shock waves through the department. They'd managed to keep it fairly quiet at the time, but a lot of managerial paperwork had come out of it. The CIA was basically trying to cover its ass, because it had been one of the worst ops in history. They had lost one of the world's worst homicidal maniacs.

Amberly would hope that after almost three years she had enough emotional distance to not be swayed one way or the other by the outcome of whatever the informant had to say, but that would be stupid. She was five hundred percent invested in the information the CI had.

When she thought about that time, when her life had quite literally fallen apart, it was full of sadness and betrayal. Loneliness. Regret. The way things had gone down had been so fast, and she'd regretted her reactions for years. It had shaped the way she did her job now, and it had been a hard lesson to learn. Be patient, and listen more than you speak. As a woman in a predominantly male world, it had been difficult to throttle her voice, even when she'd been right in her deductions. She worked with a lot of emotionally compromised men that equated a loud voice with being right.

Like her boss, Mark Brown.

The man was a letch and an asshole and every other disgusting thing she could think of. He'd made his reputation by being in a good team and taking the credit for their work. He was young for a manager, but the people who hired him seemed to love him. She just didn't understand it. The man had a line of bullshit ten miles long, but it seemed to work for him.

It was why she was here. The asshole was trying to put her off her game, so when he'd tossed the file on her desk of the botched transportation of Cole Regent and told her to figure out what had gone wrong, she'd understood he was prodding her. Brown knew exactly who her husband was, and the part he'd played. Maybe he was testing her loyalty. Again.

Operation Quicksilver had been a botched op from the beginning. She didn't understand why the Navy SEAL team had been attached as transports, because they had their own people to do that. And she didn't know why Devlin had tried to take the man out. If he'd been given orders, he would have said so. Officially, his team had been ordered to escort the target to the airport. But somewhere along the line, Devlin had chosen to take Regent out. The folder had been anemic in details, and there seemed to have been whole pages of missing info. Who had put together the op? She only knew it had come from the top levels of the CIA, which could mean any one of about twenty people. There were no orders in print. It all seemed to have been word of mouth. There should have been some kind of documentation.

Amberly doubted she would be able to magically solve the case, but she would do her best to dig up more details. Things had never settled in her mind, despite the supposed proof she'd been shown.

Most importantly, they needed to get a handle on Cole Regent. He was psychotic, literally, but he had a way about him that made him friendly and likable, and he sounded sane as he talked about the myriad government conspiracies cluttering his mind. Amberly had watched interview tapes of him, and even being in the position she was, she could understand why he would be able to sway people. Charismatic and handsome, he was capable of wreaking incredible damage. He should have been dead months ago.

When was the damn informant going to show up?

The server approached her again, a broad smile on his face. "Ma'am, I've been asked to tell you that your companion will meet you in the back courtyard."

Her stomach twisted. She wasn't sure she liked this turn. "Is the back courtyard public?"

The smiling server waffled his hand. "A little more private."

Amberly gathered her things and stood from the table, then she followed the man as he wove through the tables. In her mind she was mapping out exit strategies as she waded through people, scanning for danger. She was armed, her Springfield nestled beneath her left arm, but that would only get a single person so far, and the thought of trying to shoot her way out of a Chicago restaurant was not cool.

Following the young man through the back door, she stepped down onto a bricked floor. Immediately, her skin began to prickle, and her steps slowed. This didn't feel right. Her gaze scanned the brick walls surrounding her. There was an interior balcony along all four walls that reminded her of a place Devlin had taken her in New Orleans years ago. It was even painted white like that place. She couldn't see anyone in the depths of the rooms beyond, which was what was putting her on edge. Anyone could be standing up there, watching. Was this a kill box?

Plus, the tables were set, but not one was filled. It was as if the area had been kept witness free for a reason.

Had the CI set that up?

The man she'd traveled 700 miles to see sat in the back corner, in a shaded alcove. The table was under the balcony and in one of the most protected locations, so she appreciated that. She didn't, however, appreciate having her back to the open room. Amberly wanted to see what was going on around her at all times.

Necco, her contact, was not a very big man. Their heights were probably about even. 5'9" ish. But he was a lean man, with stringy muscles honed with strength. Brownish gray hair, with a straggly mustache. There was a hardness to his expression. Amberly knew she would not want to scrap with him because he would probably take her down.

His watery eyes darted around the space as she joined him. "You're alone, right?"

"I am," she confirmed, sliding into the seat opposite him. "Just like you told me to be. Now, what is it you made me travel up here for?"

Necco glanced around, rubbing his hands together. Then he ran his palms down the fronts of his thighs, obviously wiping sweat away. "Let me see your belly. Are you wearing a wire?"

Frowning, she lifted her shirt enough for him to see the bare skin of her belly. "Why would I wear a wire to talk to you? I never have before."

"Because I have information that will destroy your department," he hissed.

Amberly blinked, keeping her breathing steady. She'd heard things like this before, and it rarely panned out. This was likely a wild goose chase, but he had sounded determined on the phone. "Okay. I'm ready."

Amberly knew she had to wait for him to come up with the words himself. If she pushed him too hard, he would clam up and disappear. The fact that he was here now was amazing to her, because he had been the one to make contact.

Finally, he leaned toward her, over the table. "You remember Tango 11?"

Amberly's blood chilled in her veins, but she made sure

there was no reaction on her face. No civilian should know that tag. "Everyone in the department remembers him. It was one of the worst black eyes the CIA ever received."

Necco cackled, nodding his head. The manic way he was reacting made her think he was high, and the pinprick pupils seemed to back up that assumption. Everything he told her would have to be suspect.

"And?" she prompted, leaning back in the seat.

"And, he's mobilizing his paramilitary group," Necco said. "There was a small detonation outside of Bozeman. He has a new recipe, and he's sure it will work better than anything else he's had before. And he has new partners. Once he refines it, he's going somewhere east. 9-11 is next week, and he's bragging that he's going to make an even bigger impact than that."

Amberly sighed. "Necco, the man lives in Montana. All worthwhile targets are east of him. You're not telling me anything."

Necco chopped a hand in the air. "You know what I mean. He's always had it out for Washington. But he's not going there directly. He has wild ideas, Temple, and I'm not taking part in it. Something is going to happen next week, probably on September eleventh, and I'm out."

"Wild ideas like what?"

Necco blinked and glanced around. "I've done my time in prison, so I know what it's like to be without my family. Cole wants to steal families. He's looking at schools and churches, bridges, even a hospital. I ain't into that. Those people are innocent."

Amberly blinked, wondering if Necco had actually seen plans or what? "Is this written somewhere in black and white? Or are you guessing?"

He slid a blue envelope across the table to her. Amberly

was surprised because she hadn't seen an actual photo envelope for a long time. It had the name of a big box store on the front. She lifted the front flap to find a stack of grainy photos. Some were not too bad to read, others were almost useless.

"I was in a hurry," Necco said defensively, obviously understanding her scowl. "Cole stepped out for moments and I had to get the pics as quick as I could. Your fancy tech guys should be able to figure some of it out."

Amberly kept the photos in order, in case it made a difference. She stopped at one name that was actually legible. "William Taft Elementary."

"It's some random little school outside in Fort Collins, Colorado. I don't know why he picked it."

She straightened the pictures and put them back into the envelope. "Okay. And who are the new partners?"

Necco glanced around again, shaking his head. "I don't know. He talks to one on the phone all the time. Whoever this person is, though, they're ramping him up more than I've ever seen him ramped up before. It's like this guy knows exactly what buttons to push. And he has contacts with the Russians. They helped him with some of the mechanics last time."

Great. That's just what they needed. Some faceless secondary character even harder to catch than Regent. "You haven't seen the individual at all?"

Necco shook his head, which meant it probably wasn't a local boy helping out his buddy Cole. It was someone further afield.

"I need you to..."

There was a click from above them, a very distinctive click, and they both froze. Necco's eyes went wide, and he started to slide out from the table. Amberly almost told him to wait just a second, but he was already moving.

A bullet hole bloomed in the center of Necco's forehead and he went down.

Amberly dove for the brick floor, even as someone opened fire on her. He had to be behind her, toward the front of the restaurant. She'd had a perfect view of the hole in Necco's head. There was probably more than one attacker, though. It was how they usually worked.

She pulled her own weapon, then stuffed the photo envelope as far down her bra as she could. Scanning the area, she tried to see where the shooter was, then she lunged out from the alcove. A line of bullet holes appeared in front of her across the bricks, sending chips flying. Obviously, the shooter was using a silenced weapon. Crawling toward the back, she prayed she didn't get hit in the ass.

What a great story that would be at the water cooler, she thought. Shot in the ass chasing down a wild hare.

There was a door to the back, but it seemed to be locked. Of course it did. And too sturdy to break through. She swung her weapon around, praying that the envelope of pictures stayed where she'd put it. Necco was dead now, so those pictures might be the only proof she had of anything.

The doorjamb to her right splintered and she ducked, then returned fire. Her weapon did not have a silencer, though, and the shots rang loud in the Chicago restaurant. She heard people scream out in the front of the building and she prayed she hadn't struck an innocent bystander.

Then a line of blazing heat seared down her left arm, spinning her around. The pain was stunning and chilling, and it took everything she had to keep her weapon gripped in her other hand.

Something moved on the balcony across from her, so

she aimed and fired. There was a huff of air, like someone had been hit, and the movement stopped. Amberly took that moment to get out of the restaurant, escaping with the other screaming patrons. Glancing around, she caught sight of two hostiles. They were obviously watching for her, because as soon as she hit the street, they began tracking her. Even from the other side, they felt too close, and she hurried down the sidewalk, trying to hide her bleeding arm.

It was going to be obvious in a minute, because she felt the blood running down her arm. She scrambled for her phone in her hip pocket. "Fuck," she hissed, seeing the shattered screen. Useless. She shoved it back into her pocket, praying that it wasn't as bad as it looked, then looked around.

The taller man was gone.

One of the most important traits to being in the CIA was keeping a sense of calm under pressure. Her calm was unraveling, though, as the noose tightened around her.

Should she stay on the street or duck away? Listening to her gut, she ducked into the next alley, jogging along the length and to the back. There were doors along the way, but she was sure they were locked. One was open and a guy stood outside smoking. Avoiding his look she passed on. Glancing behind, she looked for her followers, but she didn't see them. Maybe they were tracking her street-side.

Then she heard two soft *pffts* of air, one right after another. A man slumped down from between two giant dumpsters, where he'd obviously been hiding, waiting for her. She looked up the height of the building, scanning for the shooter, trying to sort out in her mind who was trying to shoot her or what the hell was going on.

Her arm throbbed as she rounded a corner, bracing her

back against it. If the shooter on the roof was after her, she doubted he could shoot straight down the wall. She needed an out, though. Just then, she heard the screech of one of the L lines rumbling by. Lurching into motion, she headed for the sound. Maybe she could lose them there.

3

Dev broke into a jog, running along the roofline as he shadowed Amberly's progress.

Looking ahead, he tried to find an easy way down, because there was one more shooter he needed to get rid of. The Gods must have heard him, because within moments he found a wrought iron fire escape. He pounded down the landings, jumping when he could, until his left knee began to protest. It had been a while since he'd used it this hard. Yeah, he went jogging to maintain and he worked out, but combat situations tested you differently.

And he thought he'd been done with combat situations. He was no slouch, by any means, but he definitely wasn't in top fighting form. At his age, he didn't think he needed to be.

Amberly's life was in danger, though, and he would save her.

Scanning the area, he took off in the direction he'd last seen her running. Then he spotted the blood. It was in a long scrape, and bright red. It was obvious she'd bounced against the wall. It gave him a definite direction of travel, though. She was heading toward the L. *Good girl.*

The distinctive sound of the elevated train was straight ahead. Dev wasn't sure which line it was, but it didn't matter. It would get her out of the proximity of danger, and she could recoup her losses.

As he jogged along, he tried to imagine what it would be like to look into her silvery eyes again. It had been a long time.

Up ahead, there was a flash of movement. Picking up his speed, he headed for it. Dodging puddles of unknown substances, he did his damnedest to catch up with Amberly, but she was literally running for her life. And she'd always been faster than him. He could do longer distances, but in shorter bursts, she had the advantage.

Then the movement stopped. Dev glanced around, but he continued to move forward. Had she ducked into a hole or open door somewhere?

A garbage truck rumbled into the alley behind him, and he glanced back at it. When he looked back, Amberly stood less than fifteen feet away, the barrel of her gun pointed steadily in his direction.

Fuck.

He watched the emotions cross her face and felt like shit. Obviously, she thought he'd come after her. "Amberly," he said softly, refusing to raise his own weapon against his wife. Paperwork or not, he still considered her his wife. "I'm not here for you. I'm tracking who shot you."

She blinked, her pale eyes going hard. Her arms didn't waver in her stance, and he knew how much pain that had to cause. Fresh blood dripped from her left arm through the jacket.

"Right. Do you seriously expect me to believe that? I'm sure you were just waiting for a chance..."

Movement flickered beyond her, and Dev knew he was about to die, but... Raising his own rifle, without even lining up the scope, he fired over Amberly's shoulder, taking out the second man with a shot through the heart. He waited, breath held, for her to shoot him, but there was no sudden, sharp, burning pain. Instead, she turned to look behind. When she saw the man on the dirty alley pavement, her entire body sagged. Then she spun to look at him again.

Lowering his rifle, Dev moved to go through the man's pockets he'd just killed, and he found a wallet almost immediately. When he flipped it open and saw the CIA badge, he wasn't surprised. Amberly gasped, though, a sound she very rarely made.

"What?" she asked, faintly. "They were CIA. Were they after you?"

Dev gave her an incredulous look as he took out his cell phone and took a picture of the man, as well as the ID. "You know they weren't, babe. They were after you."

Dev twisted the barrel of his rifle, removing it from the receiver. Swinging his backpack down off his shoulders, he pulled out a hard metal case and fit the separate pieces down into the shaped foam. Close quarters like this required a smaller weapon. He snapped the lid closed, then fit the hard case into the backpack. His Beretta was in a shoulder holster, but he left it concealed under his jacket. Amberly was already spooked and he didn't want to spook her any further.

"Come on," he said, walking forward with his hand out. "Let's get out of here before someone realizes that was a gunshot and not the garbage truck making noise."

Her pale eyes flickered, and she nodded. She didn't

reach for his hand, though. Turning her back on him, she continued toward the elevated train. It shouldn't have stung, but it did.

Then Dev grinned. Yes, her pale gray eyes were as hard and calculating as he remembered. But that haircut... it was damn sexy. He'd never seen her in short hair like that, with one long wing hanging down across her face. Edgy. Made her look badass. And sexy.

They slid through the doors just in time, and Dev followed her as she headed toward the back of the car, guarding her hurt arm. The elevated cars were mostly glass, so there were no real hiding places. And they were moderately crowded, so they had to make do with what was left. The two of them garnered a few looks, but most of the watchers knew better than to dig into anyone else's business.

When Amberly chose a seat, he squeezed in beside her. "Are you okay?"

She glanced at him from beneath her lashes. "I'm fine," she snapped. "What the fuck are you doing here, Devlin?"

Scanning the car, he leaned into her shoulder. "I got a call to come to save you."

She looked at him incredulously, her eyes narrowed with pain. "Right. No one knows I'm here."

Dev looked at her askance. "Really?"

The meaning was clear. He was here, so *someone* knew she was here...

The train car rattled along the tracks, lights flashing. They were slowing for a stop, and several people were gathering their belongings.

Dev watched the people move, on high alert and ready for another attack. When he glanced over, Amberly had her weapon in her hand. Yeah, the woman could be dying and she would have a gun in her hand. Despite what was going on, he grinned at her. "I see you're just as sharp as ever."

"I see you're just as much of an asshole."

He chuckled, genuinely glad to see her. It had been a hard three years without her. He wanted to pull her into his arms and lay a huge kiss on her, but he was positive she'd shoot him if he tried. "Well, I'm a competent medic, so turn my way and I'll wrap that arm."

Amberly stared at him, hard, then swiveled in the seat as the train began to pull away from the station. "Who sent you?"

The black leather jacket she wore was trash, a bullet hole through the sleeve. But when he reached to rip it down, she pulled away and shimmied out of it, a hard grimace of pain contorting her face.

Dev couldn't help but stare. Amberly had been a strong woman before, tall and a little curvy. But at almost forty now, she was leaner, the lines of her body more sculpted. Her arms were clearly defined by muscle and it was obvious she'd honed her body to fighting readiness. Not that she hadn't been before. He allowed his gaze to drift down her chest. Man, she'd always had the nicest...

"You're such a pervert," she snapped. "Arm."

Dev chuckled, not surprised she'd caught him. "It's been a long time, what can I say? You look really good to me, Amberly. You always have."

She scowled, looking out the window, and held her arm out expectantly. Dev swung his pack around, rooting around for the first aid kit he'd packed. The wound was just a flesh wound, but it definitely needed stitches. Not something he could do on a rattling, swaying train. As soon as they got to a stopping place, he could look at it again and evaluate. For now, he would just have to try to rinse the debris out and bandage it tight to control the bleeding. Amberly gasped a couple of times, but didn't say anything or try to pull away. She'd always been a hardass like that.

When he finished, he gathered up the bloody trash he could and bundled it into a plastic bag. They were pulling into another station, and he knew they would have to get off soon. "Do you have a car?"

"Yes."

He could hear the worry in her tight voice. She knew as well as he did that the car could now be a trap. If the CIA tracked her to Chicago using either her phone or vehicle, she needed to get rid of those things. They could get replacements.

Amberly shifted in her seat and pulled a cell-phone from her pocket. Dev could see the shattered screen. He doubted it would even power on. She pressed a couple of buttons and nothing happened. It was probably for the best. They needed to remove the sim card and toss the whole lot anyway. If the CIA was tracking her, that was the easiest way to do it.

"Let's leave the car. I have my truck to get out of the city."

"No. I need to get my bag."

Dev blinked, looking at her incredulously. "You need your bag?"

She didn't even shift under his scrutiny. "Yes."

What on earth was worth her life to retrieve? They were literally running for their lives, and she wanted to stop for clothes. Whatever. He would back her play.

"Who knows you're here?" he asked instead.

Amberly pulled in a breath. "My boss, of course."

"Old Hatchett?"

She shook her head. "No, Brown. I wish it was Hatchett,

but he retired. This punk ass thinks he knows the best use of my time, which is investigating cold cases."

Devlin made a face. They were pulling into another station and they were going to have to move soon. "Seriously? You're one of the best investigators the CIA has."

Amberly sighed. "It'd be nice if someone told Brown that. Apparently, he thinks three years is enough time to have passed for me to regain my objectivity and start over at the beginning to find out who sold us out."

Devlin lifted his brows at that. "And is it enough time? Have you gotten over us, Amberly?"

Her hard eyes narrowed on him. "Completely."

Then she got up and moved toward the opening car doors, not waiting for him.

Devlin grinned for the first time in a long time and got up to follow her.

4

Her arm was a dull throb, but Amberly refused to stop. She had to get to the car, then find alternate means of transportation out of the city. At least it was her weak arm. If it had been her gun arm, that would have been harder to deal with.

Glancing at Devlin out of the corner of her eye, she wondered yet again what the hell was going on. Why had he turned up just in time to save her? More importantly, who had sent him? She had so many questions, but it wasn't a good time to talk about it. They needed to be on the lookout for whoever had tried to take her out. Because that was what that had been. An organized hit. Necco had been the main target, but she had a feeling she was to be the bonus. Necco was dead. He'd died to give her the photos tucked against her chest, and now she had to figure out where a madman was hiding while trying to keep herself alive from her own agency.

Piece of cake.

And did she really know that Devlin was here to rescue her? Considering their history, maybe he was running the op and took out his companions so that they would no longer be witnesses. No, he wouldn't work with the CIA. Wasn't his style.

Her mind was spinning, and it wasn't because of the blood loss.

Devlin could still be on the take. Three years ago, he'd been more than happy to toss their entire marriage and his career out the window for a little money. Was he still driven by cash? She had no idea what to think.

And she wasn't going to fall for the flirty vibe he had going. If he wanted to walk in here and pretend to save her, that was fine, but she was keeping her wits about her.

Man, he looked scrumptious, though.

Devlin had always been a good-looking man, and the past few years had put a fine finish on him. His hair was grayer now, but still looked thick and full, swept back from his strong forehead. It was longer than the standard SEAL cut, but it suited him. His eyes were clear and direct, a pale whiskey brown slitted against the sun. Maybe there were a few more lines at the corners, but they all had those. Even as she thought it, he retrieved a pair of sunglasses from his breast pocket and slid them on.

The man walked beside her with the loose-hipped grace he'd always had, and from what she'd seen, there wasn't a spare ounce of flesh on him. She hadn't expected him to go to pot over the past three years, but she also hadn't expected him to be in such exceptional shape. Nothing seemed to have changed. He wore black BDUs cinched low around his hips and a gray T-shirt, and the ubiquitous boots. For as long as she'd known him, Devlin Kreed had worn a single type of boot- what was currently on his feet.

It was obvious from the bullet holes in her attackers that his shooting sense was still intact, as well. What had he been doing for the past three years? Mercenary work? Black ops? He had been too good of a sniper not to use his skills after he was washed out of the Navy.

Devlin had specialized in weapons. There wasn't a gun made in the world that he didn't know about. She had a feeling she could ask him even now who was on the cutting edge of deadly weapons, and he would be able to tell her. But it had gone beyond book knowledge. His physical prowess with anything put into his hands was legendary. She knew because she'd been talking to one of his former teammates not too long ago, and he'd still been amazed at some of the shots Moon Devil had taken to protect their team, or forward the mission. He'd been such a phenomenal weapon himself.

Amberly refocused on her surroundings. There were a lot of people on the streets, but then, this was Chicago. No one paid attention to them, though. Since this L platform was on the outskirts of the city, there were a lot of people heading in one direction, toward parking. They merged into the light traffic, Devlin on her wounded side.

"This had better be worth it," he warned her, glancing around surreptitiously.

They circled the parking lot twice to make sure no one was around her vehicle. Nothing looked out of the ordinary. "You go high and I'll get my shit," Amberly told him, and Devlin nodded, separating from her. He walked casually toward an elevated parking garage next door, and she gave him a minute to get into position before she moved toward the car. Out of an abundance of caution, she reclined on the concrete to scan the undercarriage. Nothing looked out of place or abnormal. No pipe bombs or obvious tracker boxes. They might be leaving the car for no good reason.

For the slightest, barest second, she allowed her head to

rest on the concrete and closed her eyes. Tiredness made her bones ache, and she couldn't wait to get somewhere relatively safe. Then she could think and plan and decide what to do.

Levering to her feet, she looked through the windows. Nothing appeared wired, so she hit the key fob unlock and waited to blow up. When nothing happened, she scrambled to open the door. It wasn't until she dragged in a breath that she realized she'd been holding it. Nothing had happened. Leaning in, she retrieved her computer bag, then popped the trunk to retrieve her backpack. Then, shoving stuff aside, she got down into the spare tire well and retrieved a small, beaded bag. It had an elephant on the front and was worn with use, she'd had it so long. Tucking the bag into the backpack, as well as the envelope of pictures, she dropped her shattered phone into the wheel well. Then she locked the car and walked away, dropping the keys into a trash receptacle.

Devlin met her at the exit ramp to the parking garage, driving an older model Chevy truck. It was obvious it had been lovingly cared for, in spite of its age, and she felt bad for the owner. They had to get out of the city, though. Her safety trumped random-guy's possession.

"So, where are we going?" Devlin asked eventually. "I'm happy to drive and hope we find something, but I figure you have a destination in mind."

She sighed, wondering how much she should share with him. They needed to talk before she exposed all her secrets. "Head toward Peoria. We'll get a motel there and get some sleep."

"Will do."

Within ten minutes, they were cruising through corn fields, occasionally broken up by soy bean fields or solar panel fields. Amberly was not the type of person who would enjoy this area for any length of time. Give her a nice cabin in the woods... they used to dream about building a cabin and living out their lives there.

"How did you know where I was," she asked eventually.

Devlin snorted, propping one hand on the steering wheel. "Well, I had this random woman call me and offer me a large amount of money to come rescue you."

"Because we know money is your main motivation in life..." she couldn't help but murmur.

Devlin tossed her a look. "Right..."

"So, who was she with?"

"I have no idea," he sighed.

She turned her head to look at him. "So, you traveled how many miles to a place you thought I *might* be? To rescue me?"

Nodding once, Devlin glanced in the rear-view mirror before merging left to get around a semi. "And I'm glad she called, because you might have been dead if I hadn't gotten there when I did."

Amberly swiped a hand through her hair, tucking it behind her ear. "What else did she tell you?"

"That Regent was free again and about to wreak havoc. And that I, we, needed to take him out."

Amberly blinked, wondering if that was actually what he'd been told. "What did she promise you?"

Devlin glanced at her, but she couldn't see his eyes. "That my record would be cleared."

Empathy clogged her throat because she knew how important the Navy had been to him, and it made her angry. She had no business worrying about his emotions. Not after he'd ruined their entire life. She'd been interrogated for weeks after his defection, and people still, to this day, looked at her like she had betrayed the team. She had done no such thing, but she'd been painted with Devlin's guilt. It had made going to work hell on earth, feeling the stares and the hearing the snide comments as she walked by. It made her work that much harder to clear her name, and her record for solving cases and completing assignments had improved. She'd taken the chance to get out of the country as often as she could.

In the end, it had strengthened her, emotionally and professionally. Not that she wanted to live through it again. Fuck, if people knew she was with Devlin right now, she'd be under investigation again. The thought hollowed out her stomach.

It had completely gutted her to make him leave, but in her heart, she felt like she had no other option.

"Do you really think it will?" she asked, returning to the topic. "You do not know who this woman is, so you might be doing all this for free."

Devlin's jaw clenched and his skin flushed. "You may be right. But even if it falls through, I was there when you needed me."

Amberly shook her head, wishing she could be anywhere but here. This entire situation was fucked, and she didn't dare believe him that saving her was the most important thing. He didn't care anything for her. And she didn't understand why he was saying otherwise.

And had that actually been a CIA badge? She didn't recognize the man's name, Thomas Folazzo, but that didn't mean anything. The CIA was a huge agency, and they had a huge turnover throughout the departments.

What the fuck was the CIA doing trying to take her out? She was trying to find Regent. Didn't they all want to get the man dead before he killed innocent civilians?

Pulling her bag to her lap, she dug inside, finding a pill bottle. She shook out several Advil, then found the bottle of water in the side pocket. Cracking the seal, she washed the pills down, then drank down most of the bottle, her mind racing.

Maybe she should just go along with what Devlin wanted for now, because if he was going to take out Regent she needed to be there. And he needed backup.

How the hell did she get herself into these situations?

"Do you have any idea where Regent is?" she asked him, watching his face.

"Charley said upper Midwest. Montana, probably."

"Charley is the woman," she said to clarify.

"Yes," he confirmed.

Amberly thought about what he'd told her. Montana lined up with the intel they had, as well.

Supposedly.

Now she was looking at everyone as if they had betrayal in their heart. But then, there was a corrupt faction in the CIA. In her division specifically. The fact that she'd been targeted attested to that. And the fact that Regent was still alive attested to that. Who had hidden that he was alive?

It could just be incompetent management, trying to advance their careers at the cost of public safety.

Maybe her investigation was making someone worry and they'd lashed out.

She hadn't really done anything yet, though.

Her mind went in circles as she thought about the details she knew, and the holes she was aware of. Devlin drove like he could go for hours. And he probably could. The man had the determination of an ox. It was one of his greatest attributes.

Shit! Why was she thinking about his fucking attributes?

The man had betrayed her. Period. He'd betrayed the country. Most importantly he'd betrayed his SEAL team. Those men had meant everything to him, because he hadn't had a big family growing up. She remembered more than a few times, Devlin coming home tired and beat up, but shining in a way she couldn't explain because his team had done well. And because he'd been able to protect his team. She'd asked him once if it was hard to kill random people. He'd looked at her for a long moment before shaking his head. "When it comes down to it," he'd told her softly, "it's my responsibility to make sure those kids make it home. It doesn't matter what I have to do. I'll make sure it gets done."

Moon Devil. That's what his call sign had been, because he preferred to hunt in the shadow of the moon. He was a damn legend in military circles.

That had been almost ten years ago now, back when they'd first gotten together. His answer had told her the kind of man he was. Which was why his later betrayal had shocked her to the core. Devlin loved his country and his team, and there was no way he would have betrayed them.

Her mind raced, trying to ferret out an answer that had been nagging at her. Before she could grab it, Devlin put the blinker on to exit the interstate. Damn. That was a quick trip.

Devlin pulled up in front of a chain motel, not too expensive and not too cheap, and parked the truck. "I'll be back."

She didn't say anything, just watched him walk into the lobby of the motel. He was limping just a little on his left leg and she wondered what he'd done to hurt it.

"It's no fucking business of yours," she snapped at herself, falling yet again into the worried-wife role. She was not that person anymore!

When he climbed back into the truck, he avoided her look. Which made her suspicious. "You did get two rooms, right?"

Devlin grimaced and backed out of the parking spot. "No, I did not. We'll be safer together."

Anger burned through her, and it took everything in Amberly's soul not to yell at him. "I'm not staying with you, Devlin. There's no fucking way."

He spun the wheel of the truck as he backed into a parking spot on the opposite side of the motel check-in. Amberly knew he did it to protect the plate of the truck, as well as make it easier to pull away from the building in a hurry.

"I already rented the room, and I don't have enough cash to get a second one. It's a done deal, Amber. Don't worry, there are two beds."

Without another word, he got out of the truck and headed down the walkway to room 114. Ground floor, away from vending machines. Perfect positioning.

For several seconds, she just sat there, trying to control her anger. Three years ago, she would have been okay with his overhanded way of doing things sometimes. It wasn't okay now. She followed him into the room, dropping her bags to the bed closest to the bathroom. She dug a change of clothes from her backpack, as well as a small cosmetics bag, and disappeared into the bathroom. She locked the door very firmly behind her, hoping he felt the burning bubble of rage she was fighting to control.

5

Dev knew that look. Amberly was so pissed right this minute. If he gave her some time under hot water, maybe she would cool off.

At least, that's how it used to play out when he pissed her off when they were married. It seemed like that had been eons ago, though. There was a hardness to her that hadn't been there before, and he could only feel responsible. More than once he'd tried to imagine being in her shoes after he'd left. It had to have been incredibly hard, dealing with the public and private backlash. Her dad would probably never forgive him, even if he did manage to take out Regent and save the country.

The pipes rattled in the bathroom, and he hoped she was relaxing. Moving to the door, he peered through the curtain at the window. The motel he'd chosen had been a little busy, next door to a bustling truck stop. It wasn't cheap enough to rent by the hour, but it probably saw its fair share of nighttime business. Even as he watched, a woman in a super short, skintight pink dress walked across the parking lot, holding the arm of an older gentleman. Someone toward the corner of the building blared music pretty loud, and he had a feeling the cops patrolled through here fairly frequently. Once it quieted down a little, he'd swap plates on the truck and decide on a new mode of transportation.

A dark grey Dodge Charger rolled by, bass thumping, and he grinned. What better way to blend in than to look like a cop?

Amberly came out of the bathroom a few minutes later, wearing a white tank top and a pair of black athletic pants. Her short, dark hair was a cap against her head. It used to be long, and beautiful, curls down around her shoulders. "Why did you cut your hair?" he asked impulsively.

She didn't even flick him a glance. "It was in my way."

Rolling her dirty jeans and panties into a bundle, she stowed them in her backpack. Dev saw her arm was bleeding again. "Let me get that for you." He retrieved the first aid kit from his own bag, and a washcloth from the bathroom. "Sit down."

Dev knew he was pushing his luck. He could still feel the anger rolling off her, but she did as he asked, sinking to the side of her bed. "It probably needs a couple of stitches," he told her softly.

"I know. Just do it."

Dev had seen men in combat scream like little girls, but as he threaded the needle through Amberly's ripped flesh, she never uttered a word or sound. Sweat beaded on her brow and rolled down the side of her face, and there was a tenseness to her, but those were the only reactions to what he was doing. He tried to be gentle, but no matter how gentle he was, there were a few stitches that had to go deep. She gasped once and turned her head away, panting raggedly. At one point, she swayed and he worried she was going to pass out, but she didn't.

The woman had balls of steel.

After stitching and bandaging, he handed her a couple of antibiotic pills. They were his from a year ago when he'd sliced his hand open with a box knife, but he would share them with her. It had been a spur-of-the-moment decision to throw this little kit together, and he was very glad he had.

As soon as he was done cleaning her arm, she curled up on the bed and pulled a pillow over her head. Dev smiled, shaking his head. She'd always slept like that.

"I'm going to shower."

There was a noise from beneath the pillow, but he knew she would be out by the time he returned.

Dev took a few extra minutes to soak his own body under the hot water. Maybe he needed to take his own dose of ibuprofen. He wasn't used to running around like this anymore. He'd gotten used to his easy security job, and telling people what to do for him.

Cliff hadn't been happy about being left in charge last minute. "I don't know anything about the Allen contract."

"I know," Dev sighed. "But this is a family emergency."

That had stunned his buddy. "I didn't realize you had family. You've never talked about them."

"Ex-wife," he admitted. "She's in a bit of trouble. I need to go help her out."

"Okay, Dev, but this had better mean a raise."

Devlin had laughed at the time, but Cliff was definitely worth his weight in gold. When he got back, they would talk about money.

After toweling off, he left the steamy bathroom. Amberly hadn't moved. He hadn't expected her to. It was a shock to the body to be shot, even in the arm, and it took a while to recover. Yes, it was just a flesh wound, but it would hurt like hellfire tomorrow when it started to heal.

Dev dressed in a change of clothes and sat at the table, opening his rifle case. The rifle, an SR 25 7.62 x 51, was a good rifle, comparable to what he'd carried in the SEALs. He'd had to turn his favorite rifle, Requiem, in when he'd left, and that had hurt the most. That weapon had saved so many lives, and he hoped whoever ended up with it used it with the same success he had.

After cleaning the rifle and tucking it away for its next use, he catnapped, handgun on his lap, just in case. They were probably safe enough here, but there was no way he was getting caught with his pants down, so to speak. A little after three a.m., he sauntered down the quiet walkway of the motel, scoping out vehicles. The Charger was his top choice, if it was still here in the morning. More than likely his truck had been picked up on cameras, and it was probably best he left it here. If they made it out alive, he could come get it later.

Pulling a multi-tool from his pocket, he swapped plates between his truck and another, similar truck. The models were off by a couple of years, but if a cop ran the plates, it would take them a while to figure out the mess. Then he headed back to the room.

He wasn't surprised to be looking down Amberly's gun barrel yet again as he let himself into the room. "It's just me."

"What are you doing? You almost ate a piece of lead. Again."

He grinned at her. "So glad you aren't inclined to shoot me now."

She shook her rumpled head and tucked the weapon beneath her pillow. "You might be surprised how easy it would be," she warned. Turning, she laid on the mattress again and curled up into the fetal position.

More than anything in the world, Dev wanted to lay down behind her and spoon her the way he used to. They had fit together so well...

Instead, he turned the chair to lean against the wall and rested his gun on his thigh. No one would be coming through this door tonight. Resting his head against the wall, he closed his eyes.

6

Amberly woke in the most pain she could remember having for a long time, and the smell of cheap motel coffee in her nose.

The sun was up, but it seemed foggy outside. A result of being near the Illinois River, perhaps?

She blinked, trying to decide what had woken her. Must have been Devlin, stuffing items in his bag. "We need to get out of here soon," he murmured, voice raspy from disuse. "There's a Charger down the way I'll snag us."

"Okay," she said, clearing her throat. "Let me go pee and get dressed."

And take a buttload of ibuprofen.

Within about ten minutes, they were ready to go. Amberly slung her bags over her good shoulder and made sure her gun was secure in her shoulder harness. There was no telling what the owners would do when Devlin broke into the car. "Are you sure you can hotwire it?"

Incredibly, he grinned at her over his shoulder and held up a key fob. "No need."

"How the fuck did you do that?" she hissed, but he kept walking.

There was a small chirp as he unlocked a dark grey vehicle, then slid into the driver's seat. Amberly tossed her own bags into the back seat and slid in, pulling the seat belt across her chest. Her arm throbbed as she tried to fasten the belt. Devlin finally took the clasp from her and snapped it in.

"We haven't even talked about where we're going," she groused.

Devlin spun the wheel and pulled out of the motel parking lot, merging into traffic. Within a mile, he was on a westbound on ramp. "Well," he said eventually, "I know Regent is partial to his Montana roots. It's where all his paramilitary friends are. It's what he's used to."

His reasoning was sound, and it was probably the same deduction she would have made. "Actually, we need to go to Fort Collins, Colorado."

Devlin glanced at her, obviously waiting for details, and she realized she was at a crossroads. Either she trusted him and filled him in on what she'd gotten from Necco, or she tried to keep him in the dark. One way led to cooperation, and the other a long fight. She didn't feel like fighting. And unfortunately, Devlin was going to be the only backup she could call.

Did she dare message Frank, her former partner? Or did she now need to look at him as possibly one of the dirty officers at the CIA? Frank Callypso had been on the job for more than twenty years, and he knew more about the CIA than probably anyone else at the agency. It seemed like over that time he'd been through every division of the CIA, and had landed in counterintelligence and analysis. Frank thrived on gossip, he said thanks to his five sisters and growing up in Jersey. Just the thought of his heavy-featured mug made her smile. He'd been one of the few people who had stood by her when her life had fallen apart, and he had one of the most intelligent brains she'd ever met. If there was dirt in the CIA, he probably knew about it. Whether he would talk about it or not was another story.

Frank had also been one of the men tasked with escorting Regent to the airport that night. The thought made her pause in thought. It would be an incredible disappointment if he turned out to be dirty.

Brown was probably clean, even though she didn't like him. She thought about the other people in her group. Madelyn Chan was also in the cold case department, but she was older and content with where she was. She had no aspirations of moving up or out. She had been outspoken about some of Amberly's choices, but not enough to wish her ill.

Jake Dawson had been one of the most vicious in attacking her after Devlin had been implicated. She wouldn't put it past him to volunteer to come after her. Oh, man... she would love an excuse to shoot him. His buddy Brent had also been a thorn in her side. Just because they didn't like her, though, it didn't mean they were after her.

Who had the power to order teams out on hits? Her boss, obviously, and anyone above him. Was there something in the file Brown had given her that was telling? Would he have given it to her if he was the dirty one?

There were so many options to choose from.

She turned her head to look at Devlin. "I don't trust you. I just want to put that out there. If it turns out you're playing me, I will absolutely shoot you in the balls and not think twice."

He blinked his golden brown eyes, one side of his mouth cocked up. "I know that. I realize what a fucked up situation this is, but we have to work together. At this moment in time, we have no one else to rely on. Someone at the agency is trying to kill you. I think because you've come across a piece of information that will connect them to Regent. What were you doing in Chicago?"

Amberly sighed and reached back into her bag, retrieving the photo envelope. There was a smudge of brown blood on the front, hopefully hers, but the pictures themselves were fine. "Necco gave me these before someone shot him. That wasn't your bullet decorating his forehead?"

Devlin immediately shook his head. "I got there after."

She held up the stack of pictures. "This is what Necco brought me. He was with Regent up until a week ago, and he managed to get pictures of what he was working on. He's planning something for 9-11. They're not great pictures, but there are a few landmarks. One is this school, in Fort Collins, Colorado." She held up the pertinent photo. "If, by chance, he's testing out a new recipe, as Necco said, this may be a prime target."

Devlin scowled as he glanced at the picture. "At what point should we contact the FBI? Isn't domestic terrorism more their wheelhouse?"

Amberly sighed. "Yes, it is, and I'm sure the FBI is working on their own Cole Regent case. Regent is working with someone international, though. He's getting backing from somewhere. Necco hinted that he's working with the Russians again, like he did the first time. If we investigate and don't find anything right off, maybe we'll call in an anonymous tip or something. Not that they'd know what the fuck to do with it."

Devlin snorted. "Come on, the FBI is doing good right

now. They've only had seven news articles in the Post this week..."

She snorted, shaking her head. Seven was probably an underestimation. The FBI were idiots. She could hand them Regent on a silver platter and they would still fuck it up.

Well, so had we, she admitted.

It was a hard pill to swallow, being so publicly in the wrong. It was why Brown had put her on the cold cases. If he could get movement on dead files, it would prove that he was the man for the job. Personally, Amberly thought he was trying too hard to fill Hatchett's shoes. The old guy had been there for ten years and had several epic cases under his belt when he retired. Brown was trying to take a fast-track career path and make a splash.

"I really do think we're on our own," she said eventually. "As much as I would like to have backup going in to this situation, I don't know that I trust anyone enough to call them. I might call Frank at some point, but everyone else is out for themselves."

Devlin nodded again. "Agreed. If you're digging into dirty agents at the CIA, everyone will be on the defensive. You know that."

"Agreed," she sighed, eyeing him thoughtfully. "Plus, I have to work through the original investigation of how he escaped."

Devlin lifted his brows at that, then slowly shook his head. "I'm sure that'll be a page turner. I'd like to read that file myself."

She turned to look at him. "Why? So you can see all the devastation you left in the wake of your attempted hit? How do you live with yourself, Devlin? How do you live with betraying your team?"

Devlin blinked at her, and his jaw flexed. It looked like he was biting back words, but she didn't care. His actions had driven them apart, and they were still dealing with the fallout. He was supposed to have escorted Regent only, not taken a shot at him. This sniper veteran who had over a hundred confirmed kills as a SEAL had suddenly decided to turn dirty, on this particular target.

The only reason why that would have happened was if he was paid off. And it had to have been huge.

"I'd like to look at your file, all the same," he gritted out, fury burning in his narrowed eyes.

He's always hated being told when he was wrong, and this was no different.

Amberly pulled her laptop bag forward and retrieved the thick Regent file from the side pocket. These days, most of their records were digital, but the CIA insisted on having a concrete copy as well. Which meant she didn't even have to open her laptop and risk being found to research what had gone on from the time he'd hit their radar to now. It was all here. She flipped the folder open and started at the beginning.

By the time they got about halfway through Iowa, she was ready to do something else. While Devlin drove, she'd researched. The one time she'd looked up, the cornfields had lulled her into sleep. Or maybe it had been the pain in her arm. Whatever. She'd owned it and reclined the seat to sleep better.

They got sandwiches and filled up at a big gas station. "I want to drive for a while," she told Devlin, and without a word, he handed over the keys.

Within minutes, he was reaching for the file folder. "May I?"

Everything in her rebelled at allowing him access to the top secret information, but she had to do something. And she had to trust someone.

Her stomach twisted at the thought of him betraying her again, but she forced herself to breathe through it. She gave him a nod.

Devlin read quietly for a long time, quietly pulling a pair of reading glasses from somewhere. Occasionally he chuckled or hummed under his breath. Then he hit the center section and began to ask her questions.

"Why would they plan it this way," he asked, then turned to wait for the answer. She answered half a dozen questions for him before he reached the end of the folder. "Seriously? That's it? There's nothing in there about..." he paused and shook his head, tossing the file onto the backseat.

"Don't mess it up," she snapped.

Devlin went quiet, staring out the window. He didn't say anything to her for a long time, so she turned on the radio. Tucking her sore arm against her side, she focused on driving. Traffic wasn't bad and she found a Mustang cruising along at almost ninety. That would have suited her fine, but as soon as she slipped in behind him, he slowed down, thinking she was an unmarked law enforcement vehicle. "Damn it," she huffed, swinging around him. She would just have to set her own speed, she supposed. With a throaty rumble, the Charger took off when she pressed the gas.

"Don't get a ticket," Devlin said, giving her a sideways glance.

Amberly snorted. "Right..."

Devlin retrieved the package of pictures and started sorting through them. "Your dead guy wasn't much of a photographer."

"No, he wasn't, but he tried. And what he photographed seemed important to him, so we have to figure it out."

Devlin pulled one from the stack. "This is the school we're going to?"

"Yes," she said, flicking a glance at his hand. "It's the only William Taft Elementary in a five hundred mile radius from him."

"Do you think this girl goes there?" He held up the picture of the child.

That one haunted Amberly. The girl must be a target, but she couldn't say why exactly. Maybe she was the daughter of someone Cole wanted to pressure. Necco had deemed her important, and they needed to figure out why. Dressed in a plain blue T-shirt and blue jeans, the kid seemed normal, her dark blond hair drawn back into a ponytail. She wasn't smiling, though. It was like someone told her to stand against the wall, and she didn't like the person, because there was a distasteful expression on her face. "I don't know," she said eventually. "I do know she's a focus of Cole's, either a target's daughter or relative, maybe? Someone he can use to leverage?"

"Hm..."

There were a few pictures of a brick building, but there were no identifying marks that she could see. It looked like a million other brick buildings across the country.

"There are oaks and maples and tulip poplar in these pictures, so it has to be the eastern part of the country."

Amberly rolled her eyes. She'd come to the same conclusion.

"Look at the printed papers. What do you see?"

Devlin flipped through the pics till he found the ones she meant. He looked at them for a long time, turning the picture this way and that. "I'm not sure. I think I see a scribbled name on this one because it looks capitalized, but I can't make it out. This one looks like a spider with seven arms. I do see 'we'll lose the window' on this one, but it's too blurry on top. This one," he said, holding one of the pictures up at eye line, "makes me think bad vacation photo in a museum or something."

Amberly looked at the picture again. She hated to admit it, but she saw that as well. "A Washington museum?"

He made a face. "Not sure. Maybe it's the lighting or something."

After scanning the pictures again, Devlin put them back into the envelope, then set it with the operation folder on the back seat.

"We know Regent has an axe to grind against authority," he said thoughtfully.

"And the government."

Devlin looked out the window thoughtfully. "How was he apprehended the first time?"

Amberly snorted. "Well, he blew himself up. The package detonated before he had a chance to get it into position."

Devlin turned to look at her. "And what was he trying to blow up at the time?"

"A church, across the river from D.C. in Arlington, Virginia. His group had already killed thirteen people, mostly women and a few children, at an assault weapon protest the day before with a remotely triggered device."

He sat back in the seat, elbow resting near the window and hand propped against the upper door. For a moment, Amberly couldn't draw her gaze away from the picture he presented. Devlin Kreed had meant everything to her once upon a time, and it was a shock to have him in her life again so suddenly.

They'd been each other's sounding boards. They'd met years ago at a military function. Usually the CIA and Navy didn't cross paths much, but they were being recognized for a joint operation. It had been the brass's way of showing off their toys, and it was tedious in the extreme listening to bureaucrat after bureaucrat claim great accomplishments like they had actually been on the field. Devlin had been at the bar and supposedly he'd seen her walk in. Within about a minute, she had a drink in her hand and a cute Navy SEAL was smiling at her across the room.

They'd been inseparable ever since. Yes, there were some organizational issues they had to overcome. Each had secrets they couldn't share, but they'd worked it out and managed to dance around those subjects.

She hadn't known that Devlin was going to be escorting Regent that night, or that he was going to try to take him out. In the bigger scheme of things, yes, Regent was a piece of homicidal shit that needed to die, but she couldn't sanction his death in cold blood. It had shocked her when she'd learned what had happened.

And when she'd confronted Devlin, he hadn't tried to defend himself. He'd just taken the charge on the chin and accepted everything that had rolled at him.

Why *hadn't* he defended himself?

That had always nagged at her, and she wasn't sure why she was so centered on it right now. Yes, Devlin was a sniper, but he had a code that he lived by. He didn't shoot at everyone, willy nilly. There was a method to his madness, and he always followed orders.

So, why would he *not* follow orders?

If his team was in trouble, he would not take the shot. Or if he thought it would cause more problems. Or if he thought she was in danger.

Her mind focused on that last one. That felt right. Had someone threatened her, or her job, to get him to submit?

Fuck...

Amberly looked at her former husband and wondered if she'd royally screwed up. Had *she* been the one that had ruined their relationship?

7

D ev knew that something had changed in Amberly, but he couldn't pinpoint exactly what it was.

Fort Collins was a thirteen hour drive from Peoria. Dev didn't mind driving it, but he let Amberly take a turn when she wanted to, even though he worried about her arm. She didn't have the same range of motion, but she swore she was okay to drive. So, he let her, and he researched. Or caught up on his sleep.

Once again, he tossed the folder of information onto the back seat. He'd gone through it three times, and what he wanted wasn't in there. It had been a secret, covert team of CIA that had given him his orders. The only group that had that kind of power was SAC.

The Special Activities Center was the special group within the CIA that did the serious covert and paramilitary operations. They were clandestine, usually only taking part in tasks the US did not want to be associated with. There were two groups within SAC, the Special Operations Group for paramilitary operations and a second group- the Political Action Group- that took covert political action.

Considering who Regent was, Devlin could see either SOG or PAG throwing him under the bus. It didn't actually matter which group it was. It was all SAC. Which was why there was nothing about the orders in the folder. The SAC group had an incredible amount of leeway to do what they felt was right for the country. No matter who it hurt.

Surely they had been the ones responsible for moving Regent that night? And they would be just as responsible for losing him.

This time he would take him out, and he wouldn't miss.

It seemed to take them years to get through Nebraska. There wasn't much out there to look at, so Dev took the time to catch up on his sleep. The past three days had been nonstop running, trying to get to Amberly to keep her safe. And now they were on a wild goose chase, hoping that this school they were going to could tell them something. They had less than a week before 9-11, so they needed to get out there.

He was tired of sitting in the passenger seat doing nothing. After a few miles, a rest area sign flashed by. "Can you pull in there? I need to walk and stretch my legs."

Without saying a word, Amberly did as he requested. They slid into a parking slot and Dev climbed out. If he had more time, he would maybe even consider jogging the area. But instead, he took off in a broad-stride walk, from one end of the lot to the other, then back again. Amberly leaned against the car hood in the sun, her short dark hair blowing gently in the breeze. She watched him, a gentle smile on her face.

After about twenty minutes, he visited the facilities, then returned to the car. "I'm ready. Mind if I drive?"

She nodded, handing him the keys. "I'm going to use the bathroom. Back in a minute."

Dev watched her go, her body movements fluid in spite of the time in the car. He could tell she was guarding that left side, though. Locking the car, he crossed to the vending machine building and got them a couple of bottles of water, then returned to the car.

Amberly walked toward him, and it took everything in Devlin to remember that they weren't together anymore. Had she gotten with anyone since they'd been apart? He supposed technically she could have, since they weren't married, but he hoped she hadn't.

As she settled into the passenger seat, he watched her move. There was a grace and a collectedness to her he missed seeing, even when she was in pain. She'd been the only one for him for a long time, and he had a feeling she still was.

He took the buckle from her and snapped her seatbelt in, then he motioned for her to open her hand. When she did, he dropped several ibuprofen into her palm. "There's a fresh bottle of water there."

Rather than watch her struggle, he twisted the cap off the bottle and handed it to her. She drank down the pills. "Thank you very much. It burns like fire right now."

"I bet," he murmured.

He'd been shot before as well, but sometimes a through-and-through was better than a long slash through flesh like she had.

Backing the car out of the slot, Devlin headed for the interstate. They were only about three hours from Fort Collins.

"I'm wondering if I should call Frank," she said suddenly, turning the radio off.

"Callypso?" Dev glanced at her to clarify.

"Yes, just to let him know I'm safe and not dead."

Dev didn't say anything for a few long moments. He was aware that Amberly considered Frank her mentor, but he'd never really liked the guy. It was like he tried too hard to be personable, or something. "I suppose it's up to you, but it's an incredible risk. Right now, we're flying dark. As soon as you reach out, they'll tag us, you know that."

Amberly scowled. "You're right, of course. I just didn't want him to worry."

"I think he'll forgive you once he hears the circumstances. Let's check out a couple of things, first."

"Okay," she sighed. Then she shifted in the seat, her gaze focused on him. "Why did you try to take Regent out that night?"

Dev looked at her. There was a belligerent expression on her face, and he wasn't sure anything he said would change her mind. "It doesn't matter."

Anger sparked in her silvery eyes and she swiped her hair back. "Yeah, I guess it doesn't."

She turned and looked out the window, then she grabbed the photo envelope and started going through them again.

Devlin was very aware of her movements, just like he'd always been. When he'd first met her, he thought she was too hard. At the time, he'd been in the SEALs almost ten years, and he was kind of thinking about settling down. Or building a life outside of the Navy. The grind was wearing him down, and he knew there would be repercussions for the life he lived.

So, he'd started seriously looking at women, more as possible companions than bed buddies. Amberly had a strength to her he'd never seen in a woman before, and it had sparked something in him. Some need to meet her, head on. They'd had some of the most amazing fights, and even more amazing sex. She could spar with him as well as any of his teammates, and she gave him a run for his money when it came to shooting. The woman was sharp and confident, intellectual, and she made him want to be a better man. Amberly Temple had a love for her country that was quiet and unyielding, and she showed that love through her dedication to her job. She was the perfect overseas operative.

She also had aspects to her that she didn't show many people. Like the soft, feminine side that loved him to oblivion. And the fun side that bought her nieces and nephews bubbles to blow outside on a freezing day. And the tomboy side that helped her father refurbish an old tractor.

All of those things together had made him fall so hard. Seeing her now, sitting beside him, he wondered if some higher power was at work, trying to get them back together. Or maybe it was getting them together to save lives. He didn't know. All he did know was that he was still in love with his ex-wife.

"How are your mom and dad doing?"

Amberly glanced at him. "Fine. Dad's showing a little more wear and tear, but Mom is the same as ever. Nothing slows her down."

Dev snorted. "She'll be going that speed til the day she dies."

"Probably." Amberly grinned. "Sloan and Peach had a miscarriage a while ago. They've been trying to have kids, and it's not working."

"Damn. I'm sorry."

Sloan was Amberly's younger brother by about five years. He and his high school sweetheart Priscilla, who everyone called Peach, made one of the most right couples Devlin had ever seen. It was like they were two halves of a whole. They complemented each other so well.

"Scarlett is going into fourth grade and Scout is in sixth grade now."

"Wow," he laughed. "It seems like days ago they were just babies, and Trista was fretting over everything. Remember when Scout was born, she wouldn't let anyone in the house other than your mom? Because we were around criminals all day," he shook his head. "And Rand backed her up on everything."

"Well, he loved her. Still does. He's making noises about another baby, but I don't think Trista is going for it."

"Well, she can be as stubborn as you," Dev laughed, "so Rand might be in for a fight if he really wants it."

They shared a smile, then Amberly seemed to realize what she was doing, and she turned away to look out the window. "They all missed you when you left," she said softly.

Dev's heart stuttered in his chest. "And I missed them," he admitted, throat going tight.

And he had. The Temples had been more of a family to him than he ever could have hoped, and the thought of walking up to Tom Temple and trying to explain to the man why he'd betrayed his daughter had made him sick to his stomach. So, he'd avoided them altogether. Well, most of them.

"I don't know how she got my address, but your mother sent me cookies and a card every Christmas," he said softly.

Amberly gave him a sharp look. "Did she really?"

Dev nodded. "And a note on my birthday."

"That sneaky woman," Amberly said, shaking her head.

Dev had appreciated it more than he could say. Lana

had been a true mother figure to him when he and Amberly had been together, and he missed her hugs more than he thought possible. The little woman was a powerhouse, and it was no wonder Amberly had turned out the way she had.

"So, where have you been?" Amberly asked.

Dev glanced at her. "Outside of Chattanooga, Tennessee."

Her dark brows shot into her bangs. "Seriously? Tennessee?"

Smiling at her outraged gasp, Dev nodded. "Yup. Been there the past couple of years. The people are nice and the temperatures comfortable."

She blinked at him. "And what do you do there?"

"I have my own private security company."

"As in, a mercenary company?"

He gave her an incredulous look. "No. I wire cameras and surveillance systems. Usually to catch employee theft. No guns, no killing people."

"I had to ask," she said defensively.

It was aggravating to him she thought so little of him, that he might go out and kill for money. It hadn't been a job he'd ever wanted, it had just suited his skill set. He liked guns and he was good with them. As soon as his commanding officers had seen that, they'd plugged him into a spot, and that was where he'd stayed his entire Navy career.

Now that he didn't have to kill for a living, he was a much more relaxed person. Or at least he thought so.

It was disheartening that her opinion of him had fallen so much. Of all the people that had turned on him, her ill thoughts hurt the worst.

In his heart, he knew it hurt because he was still hooked on her.

Fuck.

They didn't talk much after that, and he was fine with it. In his mind, he knew Amberly would probably never forgive him or understand what he'd done for her, and their family.

They arrived at Fort Collins an hour later, just in time for the sun to set behind the mountains. There was a single car in the school parking lot. He assumed it was a custodian, or maybe the principal, catching up on last-minute work. Dev didn't know what he was looking for, but he circled the school a couple of times.

"Do you think we should go in?" Amberly asked, leaning against the center console of the car.

Dev made a face. "Not until I've researched it a little. Let's go get a hotel room and plan. The direct approach may be a better option."

She gasped, looking at him like he'd grown a second head. "Are you serious?"

Dev looked at her and grinned. "Nothing like living life on the edge," he said, looking at her lips.

Amberly blinked, shaking her head. "You're nuts," she whispered. "And I'm not sure how on the edge you can be in a school."

Dev snorted, letting her back away. "True. I think in this instance it will be better to go in the front door."

"We'll research it and see."

8

Amberly hated to admit that Devlin might be right. They could break into the school, but with surveillance cameras and the like now, that was a difficult thing to do while keeping a low profile. Cameras were everywhere, and if she knew the CIA, they were already running programs looking for her face to pop up somewhere around the world.

Traffic cameras had probably gotten her already.

Amberly was still torn about whether she should call in. As it was, she was AWOL, and she could make several assumptions. The gunfire had probably been reported to local police, and the CIA had probably found her picture somewhere. Necco had probably chosen a fairly safe spot to meet her, but as much as she'd run outside, she had no doubt a camera had picked her up *some*where.

Maybe they had also picked up that she'd been shot and assumed she'd gone to ground.

Devlin posed a different set of problems. If she'd been seen with him, people might assume that she was back with her turncoat husband. And the CIA would then be looking for her for an entirely different reason.

Amberly hated all the questions and she knew she would have to call in at some point, just to appease her own peace of mind.

They settled on an out of the way motel. Again, he only got them one room, but she wasn't going to complain. Even though she'd catnapped all day, she could tell her body was using a lot of energy to fix her arm and she was tired. Not crazy tired, but she knew she would allow him to keep watch over her. Knowing he was there, across the room, had been entirely too comforting last night, and she'd slept like the dead. Actually, she'd slept like she had when he'd come home from deployments years ago, wrapped in his arms and safe.

Devlin had always been protective of her. As she'd grown up and settled on what she'd wanted to do in her life, she'd gotten a lot of resistance to her dreams. When she told people she wanted to protect the country at all costs by joining the CIA, she'd usually been laughed at. It had been a struggle to get people to take her seriously. It wasn't until she'd done a stint in the Marines, then gotten her bachelor's degree in international studies and had applied to the CIA before people started taking her seriously. Then she'd had a completely new demographic of people to convince — her superiors — but she'd always been up for the challenge.

Amberly loved the business of being a spy. She loved learning integral information vital to national security, and being a part of the team to act on that information. She missed it. She was in a much smaller division, now, which dealt with dead or inactive cases that hadn't had a satisfactory ending. She was analyzing data, basically. It was not where she wanted to be, but her credibility had taken a serious hit after Devlin's defection.

But Devlin had always supported her devotion to her job. Not once had he ever told her to not take a job.

"Do you mind if I shower?" she asked, her mind as tired as her body.

"Not at all," Devlin said, setting his pack on the bed near the door. He'd also carried in the folder of information, his aluminum rifle case and the envelope of pictures. "When you get done, I'd like to check your arm."

Amberly said nothing as she slipped into the bathroom. Ugh... nothing like 1970's pink tile. Dropping her clothes to the floor, she carefully untaped the bandage from her arm, then twisted to look in the mirror. Well, it looked better than it had, but it was still angry and swollen. And very hot. Maybe a cool water shower...

When she stepped out in her tank and black nylon yoga pants, Devlin was sprawled on the far bed, legs crossed and one arm under his head. His eyes were closed, but she had a feeling he was only half asleep.

Laundry was going to be a problem. Chicago was supposed to have been a two-day trip, and she was working on day four of wearing the same clothes. She'd traveled enough in her career to know that she was going to have to buy new clothes or take a couple of hours to do laundry. Neither she wanted to take the time to do.

Her gaze wandered back to Devlin, and his long form. The man could cat nap like a pro. Then her gaze drifted down, along his strong chest and down his stomach to his narrow hips. Those muscles he'd worked so hard for were still there, even though he hadn't been active for years.

A heated shiver rolled through her and she tore her gaze away. Devlin had been like catnip to her. He'd been her one true weakness, the only person who had ever managed to tap her heart. And her body had sung for him. Just thinking about all the orgasms and all the ways he'd worked her to a frenzy beaded her nipples.

"Sit down and I'll check your arm," he said, rolling up on the bed.

Amberly almost jerked, but she managed to catch herself. Of course, he was still awake. She looked down at her chest and busied herself with crossing to the bathroom to set her clothes on the counter. Think non-sexual thoughts. Maybe she could at least rinse out her shirt and panties to get them clean. She needed to clean her weapon. Maybe it would rain.

By the time she turned around, her breasts were under control. Kind of. She felt self-conscious. And flushed. She glanced in the mirror. Yep, her chest was mottled. Damn it. Last night she'd been in too much pain to even think about him seeing her boobs that exposed.

Amberly sank to the edge of the bed, and Devlin sat down beside her.

"I don't like the look of this," he said, voice deep. "I've got a few more antibiotics. I'll double your dose tonight."

"It's hot," she admitted. "I took a cool shower, but it doesn't seem to have cooled it at all."

Devlin's mouth tightened, and he cleaned the wound. Then he very carefully smeared antibiotic ointment on the wound and wrapped it in gauze.

Amberly drew in a deep breath. They'd been in the car all these hours and she'd been breathing in his scent all that time. It should have been enough, but she found herself drawing him in again since he was leaning close. He'd been in the car as long as she had, but he smelled like man, spicy and sharp. He smelled like he used to when he'd come home from deployment, worn and tired, needing to do laundry and smelling of fuel and desert and gun oil. The machinery scent had become one of her favorites, though, because it meant she was about to be wrapped in his arms. And they would welcome each other home again.

Devlin went still, and she knew why. Her nipples had gone hard again, an oh, so obvious tell that she was aroused. Having his hands on her, even just for this reason, shouldn't have made her body react. After three years it should have been gone, this weakness to his nearness. Instead, it felt like when they were dating, nervous and excited about possibilities.

Amberly had never seen herself as the woman getting married in a white dress and walking down the aisle to her businessman husband, then popping out 2.5 kids. She and Devlin had been more practical, going before a Justice of the Peace before he left on one of his deployments, and the kids, well... kids were apparently never meant to be for them. They'd tried, but...

She swallowed and backed off a little, her eyes dropping from him.

"Even hurt and in pain and trying to be a bitch, you're beautiful to me."

One of Devlin's fingers ran down her cheek. Amberly was pissed at herself because she wanted to nuzzle into that touch, like she was a starving woman. She was stronger than that, damn it! For three years, she'd taken care of herself because she had no other choice.

The stroke of his finger reminded her what it had felt like to be with him, though. Devlin had taken care of her more than any other person she'd ever been with, and he'd relished pleasing her sexually. Those hard hands that could kill and manipulate every weapon the Navy offered could so effortlessly soften on her like silk. Every single touch had meaning and promise and could lead to intense pleasure. That lone finger had started so many passionate incidents.

Amberly could see the memory of it in his gaze, as well. Devlin's Adam's apple bounced as he swallowed and glanced away. Then he looked back, the expression on his face unexpectedly vulnerable. "It's been a while, babe. Thank you for looking at me like that. It makes me think of happier times."

"Me too," she admitted. She couldn't move if her life depended upon it. Actually, she realized she was leaning a little toward him.

That was all the motivation Devlin needed, because he cupped her head and kissed the hell out of her.

Amberly hated being weak and giving in, but it had been so long since she'd been held or kissed. Or even touched. Was this just an overreaction to being near a man she knew had cared for her? After her divorce she'd been asked out, but none of them had seemed right, so she'd said no. That, of course, led to a whole new string of issues at work. She didn't mind being called cold by the men she turned down. It just supported what her intuition had been telling her when she'd turned them down.

Devlin tilted his head, kissing her deeper, and she wondered what the hell she was doing. This man had violated her trust, as well as that of so many other people. But he'd been her love, her heart, for so much longer.

He was the one to draw back, and she thought she saw a quiver in his hand as he lowered it from her face. "Proximity," he said simply.

Anger sparked in her gut. "Seriously? So, any female you got close with would have sufficed?"

He drew back, obviously startled. "Fuck, no. That's not what I meant at all. Just that, I know you wouldn't want me, specifically, touching you. I know how much I hurt you, and I'm sorry. I don't think you were open to hearing it then, but I am so incredibly sorry things happened the way they did."

Amberly struggled with all the words that wanted to spew out of her mouth. She did want to scream and rail at him, but it wouldn't do any good. It was over and done with. Right?

"Just, why?" she said, eventually. "I mean, we were making good money. We had no real bills to speak of. Everything was covered. What would make you try to take Regent out? Was it an ego thing?"

Devlin looked down at his boots, mouth pursed. "You wouldn't... It doesn't matter anymore. I don't want to talk about it."

He moved to get off the bed, and she grabbed his arm. "What the hell, dude? You ruin my life and now you don't want to talk about it? Are you serious?"

"You won't like the answers I give you," he snapped, "so you might as well float along in your little bubble as long as you can."

She jerked back. "What are you talking about? I'm not in a bubble."

Devlin snorted and pulled away. "Right. I'm going to shower."

Turning, he headed for the bathroom, snapping the door closed behind himself. Within a few seconds, she heard the water start up. Images of Devlin in the shower assaulted her, redirecting the anger he'd sparked in her. Many times, they'd showered together, just because they couldn't stand to be apart. The shower had always led to other things, which usually led back to the shower.

Snorting, she dropped back onto the bed, her throat tight and her heart thumping. Her body was betraying her, reacting to him like they'd been apart for a long deployment. It didn't seem to understand that the emotional aspect had changed.

Reaching down, she stroked her fingers over her mound, remembering how Devlin used to kiss her there. Her fingers swirled, rubbing outside the cloth, wondering if she dare reach beneath. No, he would return soon. Closing her eyes, she allowed herself to imagine, just for a moment, that it was his hands on her. Giving her pleasure the way they used to. Taking care of her the way they used to.

9

Devlin cursed when he realized he'd left his toiletries bag outside, and he opened the door.

The sight of Amberly on the bed, eyes closed, mouth open, hand rubbing at her pussy caught him totally off guard, and gave him an instant boner beneath the rough terry-cloth towel. He watched, mesmerized, as she circled, circled, her head twisting on the pillow. Then her mouth opened, and she breathed out a long breath. Her hand stilled and it seemed like she was forcing herself to stop.

"Please keep going," he murmured softly.

Amberly's eyes flew open and she jerked her hand away. She glared at him, and he knew she was going to unleash on him. He kind of didn't care, though, because the image of her masturbating was burned into his brain. He held up a hand. "Before you yell, I want to tell you, you were, are, beautiful when you do that. I've always thought so." He nodded to his towel, tented straight out. "I'm more than willing to join you, and take care of the itch I think we both have."

For a moment, her silvery eyes softened with need and

she opened her mouth. Then she seemed to realize what she was doing, and her expression closed down. "I don't think that would be a good idea."

Dev wasn't surprised that she turned him down. It had been a wild swing for a home run, and she'd shut him down. That was okay, though. He'd learned something invaluable.

Crossing to the other bed, he grabbed his toiletry bag, letting the towel come apart. He held it and the toiletry bag in his hand, and turned, letting her get an eyeful of the heavy erection he was sporting. Then he fisted it for good measure. Her eyes glazed over, and he knew she was fighting herself at that moment. "I'm going to go jack off in the shower, and let you have fun out here, but remember, I could have fucked you better than your fingers."

He walked back toward the bathroom, until she called his name.

"Devlin," she paused, looking torn. Then she shook her head. "I can't."

Dev let himself into the bathroom, closing it tightly behind himself. He didn't lock the door, though, just in case she wanted to join him. Watching her had been... arousing, to say the least. Stepping into the weak shower stream, he let the hot water flow over him, and he poured out a puddle of shampoo into his hand. He lathered the hair on his head, then worked down his body. His dick was more than happy for the attention, and he stroked for less than thirty seconds before he came. It was a decent orgasm, but pedestrian. Balls deep inside Amberly would have been preferable.

Stepping out and seeing her rubbing her own body had been titillating. And it also gave him insight into her heart. She still wanted him. He'd seen her catch her breath when he was near, and the puckered nipples had been a dead giveaway of her sexual state. It was what had ramped him up so bad, seeing her tits so perky and needy. Had she been with anyone while they'd been apart?

Dev rinsed his hair and body, stepping out onto the damp floor towel. Then he grabbed the bath towel and dried himself as well as he could. Already, his dick was semi-hard again. He needed to stop thinking about Amberly masturbating, her long legs spread for her hand.

Wrapping the towel around his hips, he stepped out of the bathroom, eyes going straight to Amberly on the bed. She was staring up at the ceiling, hands folded over her stomach.

"I hope I gave you enough time to do what you needed to do," Dev said, feeling a little vindictive. He doubted she'd pleasured herself after he'd left. "I jacked off in the shower, but if you need anything, just let me know. I could go for a round two. I've missed your pretty..."

"Stop it, Devlin," she snapped, rolling onto her side. "We're not like that, anymore."

"I'm just offering to help you out. We know how hard it can be."

He grinned, leaving the pun for her. She huffed out a breath, but he could tell she was half-amused. "I'm going to sleep. I suggest you do too."

Devlin knew they were in a serious situation, but needling Amberly had been a favorite pastime of his. She'd get madder and madder until she finally lashed out, then they'd have glorious make-up sex. It wasn't as good as after-deployment sex, but damn close.

If they did sleep together, it was going to seriously mess with their emotions. He wasn't even sure they should, he just knew he wanted to, and she wanted to. They'd been so good together...

Besides, if they were going to die on this mission, he wanted one more lovemaking session with her.

Dev pulled on a pair of underwear and lay down upon the mattress. It was lumpy, but smelled fresh, so he climbed beneath the sheets. It was a lot better than some places he'd slept over his lifetime.

Sliding his Beretta beneath his pillow, he rolled onto his side to watch her back. There was tension in the line of her spine, and she was guarding her breaths. She hadn't fallen asleep yet.

He was very familiar with sexual frustration. It had prodded him every day since he'd been without her, and there were only so many times a man could masturbate. One session of lovemaking took the edge off better than anything, and the relaxation lasted longer. Twice he'd gone out with other women, but they hadn't appealed to him in that way. Every second they were out, he'd felt like he was cheating on Amberly.

They were divorced on paper, but not in his heart. He doubted his heart would ever give her up.

They were in a hell of a pickle right now. She thought he was a treasonous asshole, the worst thing he could be in her eyes. She was a diehard red, white and blue, and would never forgive him for violating what she held dear.

If he told her about the black ops CIA team, he wasn't even sure she'd believe him. It was such a far-fetched story.

Tomorrow, they would go figure out why this school was important. And maybe she'd take a chance on him again.

AMBERLY SLEPT LIKE SHIT. Images of Devlin climbing into the bed and making love with her plagued her sleep, and she woke suddenly with her hand down her panties, a gentle orgasm rolling over her. The room was dim and she doubted Devlin was awake, so she removed her hand and let her heartbeat and breathing settle.

This randy need was going to be the death of her. At almost forty, she should have been able to control her libido. She needed to focus on what they were here for, not her sexy ex-husband.

Images of him turning, towel in his hand and cock proudly pointing toward her flashed through her mind. How audacious was he, thinking he could flash his dick at her and they would fall back into bed together?

Was he really, though? Things had been fine until her body had reacted to his, and he'd walked out and seen her toying with herself.

What had she been thinking? How humiliating.

And now he was teasing her, flashing her with his body and saying inflammatory things meant to throw her off. It reminded her of when they were married. The man had teased her unmercifully. Devlin had always followed through with the teasing, though. The man could fuck her into unconsciousness.

Just the thought was enough to make her pause. Then the anger surged. They had a fugitive to find, damn it!

Amberly rolled out of bed and headed for the bathroom to get ready.

When she left the bathroom, Devlin was already up and dressed and packed. Amberly moved to her own bag, stuffing a few things in. "School probably starts about eight. You still want to go directly to the principal?"

"I think so," Devlin said, swinging his bag over his shoulder. He moved to the window, peering out. "We're ready."

With a last glance at the room, Amberly followed him.

ROBERT WINCHESTER SEEMED VERY young to be a principal, but who was she to judge?

Once the overly cautious receptionist let them through the locked main office door, Amberly let Devlin take the lead.

"My wife and I are scouting out schools," Devlin told the woman, grinning at her, "and we'd like to talk to the principal about a sensitive matter."

The receptionist/ office guard dog smiled at them and nodded. "If you'll take a seat, I'll see if he's available."

Within just a couple of minutes, they were hustled into a large office, and a tall young man with a frizzy shock of red hair was shaking their hands. "It's a pleasure to meet you both. My name is Robert Winchester. This is my first year as principal, but I'm sure your issue won't be anything we can't deal with."

They sat in the two chairs facing Mr. Winchester's desk and shared a look. Devlin nodded for her to take the lead.

"Mr. Winchester, we're not actually here for our child. We're following up on a lead and we need your utmost discretion." Pulling her CIA badge from her pocket, she held it out long enough for Winchester to get a good look at it. The man looked up at her blankly.

"I don't understand... You don't have a child?"

"No, sir. We're here because... well, can you tell us if you recognize this child?"

Amberly held up the picture of the little girl. Mr. Winchester took it from her, and nodded. "Yes, I know this girl."

Amberly could have sagged with relief. Finally, a break.

"But I'm not going to tell you any more until I speak with her mother."

Suiting actions to words, he reached for the phone. Reaching over the desk, Amberly stilled his hand. "Mr. Winchester. Not to be too dramatic, but we're tracking a homicidal maniac. The safety of your entire school population relies on you answering our questions. If you react in any way to our presence in the school, the person we are after will know we've been here."

Winchester sank back in his chair, brows furrowed over his blue eyes and mouth pursed. "Do you think they're in danger now?"

"I don't know," Amberly answered him honestly. "We have no idea who this girl is, just that her picture was on the desk of a convicted murderer. We don't know if it's his daughter or the daughter of someone he's trying to leverage. What can you tell us about her?"

Mr. Winchester dry-washed his hands. "This is highly unorthodox, not to mention illegal."

"I know, Mr. Winchester," Amberly said quietly. "And I appreciate your wanting to protect the children. If there's any other way we could have done this, we would have. But we have a picture of your school, and the picture of this girl from this man's desk. Now, what's her name?"

Winchester sank back into his chair. "Annabelle Jones. She started attending earlier this year and I've only met the mother, so far. She's a nice, working woman by the name of Brea. They moved here from back east, somewhere. No reason why, that I can remember."

"Are there any other family members?"

Winchester frowned. "She's talked about her grandfather, but no names."

Amberly looked at Devlin, wondering what else they

should ask.

"I think you've answered everything we needed, Mr. Winchester," Devlin said, smoothly taking up the slack in the conversation. "If you don't mind, let's keep this conversation between us. Right now, there's no obvious danger. We're just trying to suss out what they're planning. When we have more information, we'll let you know."

Devlin reached out and shook the man's hand. Amberly did the same, then walked through the office door he held open for her. They smiled at the receptionist but didn't respond when she tried to start a conversation.

They walked out to their stolen vehicle, quiet. When they settled into the car and Devlin cranked the engine, she glanced across at him. "What do you think?"

"I think he answered what we asked, and we're a little further ahead in knowledge, but not much else."

Yeah, that's kind of where she was, too. Digging in her bag, she pulled out the packet of pictures, flipping through them again. She set the one of the girl and the one of the school aside, and focused on the others. "This one keeps nagging at me," she said as she pulled one out. It was a picture of handwriting.

"It looks like a shopping list, the way it's laid out. Hold it out."

Amberly held it out, away, near the window. Devlin squinted. "Does that say wire? And maybe that second one, 9mm. Or maybe I'm just seeing what's on my brain. And does that say Zed at the top? Is that the end of a word?"

Amberly gasped. "No, it's a name, and I know that name!"

Flinging the picture to the dash, she rooted for her file on Regent. Then she started flipping through papers until she stopped on one. It was a list of known associates. Zed

Torrance was the fifth name down on the list. Triumphantly, she held the paper up for Devlin to see. He grinned, nodding.

"And now we just have to find Torrance. If he's with Regent, he'll be running errands for him. He's a low-level crook, known more for burglaries and robberies than anything else. But he's gotten arrested with Regent twice for disorderly conduct. I think they were protesting a natural gas pipeline or something, carrying AR 15s."

"Ah, yes, let's dance on the edge of death and hope no one shoots a pipeline to blow everyone up. Does Mr. Torrance have an address?"

"No, but his mother does," Amberly grinned, flipping through the papers again. "Though she's about a five and a half hour drive North from here."

"No problem," Devlin said, settling back into the chair. "That's the direction we were headed, anyway."

They fueled up at a truck stop and got on the interstate headed North. Amberly pored over the pictures, trying to figure out what they were.

"We don't have a scanner," Devlin said, "but why don't you take a picture of them with my phone and do a reverse image search."

"Oh, good idea," she breathed, grabbing his phone from the center console. Without thinking, she typed in a code. The phone opened. "You still use the same code," she laughed.

Devlin scowled and shrugged. "Yeah."

It took a few different shots, but she eventually found the correct lighting to get Google to work its magic.

"One brick building corner has no results, but the different angle of the same corner came up as... a library in Alexandria, Virginia."

"Outside of Washington, D.C."

They shared a look. If the info that Necco had given her was correct, there would be an attack at the end of this week, on the anniversary of 9-11. It was the perfect time for Regent to make a splash. Everyone would already be in front of their TVs.

"Obviously, Zed is still working for him. If we find Zed, we probably find Regent."

"More than likely," Devlin agreed. "Or maybe Zed has been given the shopping list. That's why his name is at the top."

The car accelerated smoothly onto the interstate, and for the first time, Amberly appreciated that he was here. They maybe didn't get along like they used to, but Devlin could be relied upon in a challenge. He didn't even bat an eye at needing to travel another six hours, just took the wheel and got to it. Which allowed her to brood over the pictures some more.

Another building corner came up as a coffee shop in Newport News, Virginia. She looked the place up, but it didn't seem special for any reason.

Man, if only Necco had taken better pics.

"If I could call this in, I could have a dozen sets of eyes looking at it within minutes," she sighed.

"And have the CIA breathing down your neck and trying to take Regent in. I plan on taking him out, like the CIA was supposed to do three years ago."

Amberly shook her head. "We were going to interrogate him, collect his contacts. Then stash him away. But you tried to kill him."

Devlin gave her a dark look, but didn't contradict her.

Amberly waited for some response, but he clammed up. "Why won't you talk to me?"

Devlin shook his head. "Because you won't believe me if I tell you."

She blinked, feeling a little defensive. "Try me."

"Really?"

"Yes!"

He stared at her for a long moment, mouth pursed, then turned back to watch the highway. "The CIA, I assume SAC, blackmailed me into taking the fall for the Regent hit."

Amberly's mouth fell open, then she snapped it shut. Seriously?

"Why?" she asked simply.

Devlin sighed, propping one hand on top of the wheel as he drove. "I was supposed to 'wound' him, and they would fake his death. They were going to house him in some clandestine location and milk as much info from him as they could, then they were going to dispose of him. Permanently. Imagine my surprise, when, three years later, he pops up on the radar again."

Devlin glanced at her, and he frowned, shaking his head. "I can see the disbelief in your eyes. Two men approached me with CIA identification, told me to take him out. If I did it with no fuss, they wouldn't implicate you when I was charged."

"Me," she gasped, her mind reeling. "No, wait. They played me a recording of you making a deal..."

"Did they really?" Devlin said, fury suffusing his face. "They said they would only use that recording if I didn't go along with what they wanted. Another lie."

He smacked the steering wheel with his fist so hard she worried he'd break something. Then he gripped it in both hands and yelled.

"Pull over, before you wreck us."

He jerked the wheel to the side, skimming behind

another car close enough that the woman honked her horn as she drove away. The Charger skidded to a stop on the berm and Devlin turned off the ignition. "I went along with everything they said, and they still played you that audio. That wasn't me, Amberly." Turning his head, he stared her in the eyes. "You've known that something wasn't right. Well, this is it. I was framed by your agency," he poked a finger at her chest, "and they are still fucking with my life. And fucking with your life."

Amberly stared at him, hearing the truth in his voice, but not wanting to believe it. "Why would they do that?" Her voice was faint, but he heard her.

"Because your agency is full of sanctimonious assholes who think they're God, doing what they want by any means necessary. They wanted Regent to disappear, and they needed a fall guy."

She sat back in her seat, trying to roll through the details as she remembered them. Had she been the leverage they'd needed to make him take the fall? Yes, she probably was. Holy hell.

"Who was it that came to you?"

Devlin shook his head. "Two CIA types. They showed me IDs, but I doubt they're legit. Holmes and Stacey. They could have passed for twins."

Something twanged in her brain. She knew who he was talking about. They did everything as a two-man team. The names were wrong, though. She would have to ask Frank... Or Brown. Maybe. Fuck! What was she supposed to do now? This indecision was going to drive her mad!

What Devlin said made a strange kind of sense. He'd never lied to her before. Maybe that was why he hadn't defended himself to her. Fuck, if this was true, she'd been the worst wife ever.

"So, there was no payoff..."

DEVLIN LOOKED AT HER INCREDULOUSLY. "Seriously? Have you listened to anything I said? I don't kill for money. Period. Ever. I did it to protect you!"

He was all but yelling at the end, and she didn't blame him. For three years he'd been labeled as treasonous, and no one, including Amberly herself, had stood up for him.

The isolation he must have gone through, and the loneliness. "Oh, Devlin."

Incredibly, tears started in her eyes. She never cried for anyone, but the thought of Devlin being turned on by everyone he cared about... her own family, and the few members of his... God, his SEAL team, and all of his commanding officers.

"Hell, babe, I didn't tell you this to make you cry," he said, voice gruff as he cupped her neck and pulled her close to kiss the edge of her mouth. "I never planned on telling you any of it."

"Devlin," she breathed. "I really had no idea. I knew something didn't seem right, but I couldn't put my finger on it. It's that you're as much of a bleeding heart for this damn country as I am. I knew in my heart that you taking money for a kill sounded wrong, but I was presented with 'indisputable' truth in the recording."

"Not proof. Their version of it."

"Yes," she agreed, letting her mouth brush along his own. "I'm sorry, Devlin, for not believing in you."

He kissed her then, open-mouthed and hungry, and it was one of the sweetest, hungriest kisses she'd ever been given. Her heart thudded with everything he'd told her, and she felt like the lowest of the low not to have believed him. Devlin was a good, kind man at heart, and she'd completely shoved all that aside in her blind support of her corrupt agency.

The thought of all that they'd lost. Their relationship, their marriage, the house they'd bought together. All gone.

So that the agency could have a little more information.

Anger and heartache burned through her, and she knew she had no right to enjoy his touch, his kiss, as much as she was, but she couldn't help herself. He'd been everything for her for so long, and then he was gone...

The squawk of a police siren jerked them apart and spun them around in their seats.

"Fuck!" Devlin snapped, his eyes going to the rear-view mirror. "I'm going to have to run. We have no documentation..."

Something seemed different about this stop. The cop wasn't behind them, he was pulling up the side. "No, I don't think we have to. Roll your window down."

A Wyoming State Trooper pulled along beside them. "You folks all right?"

"Yes, sir," Devlin said immediately, forcing a smile. "I apologize. We haven't seen each other in three years and I had to kiss her."

The trooper laughed and waved a hand. "Interstate isn't the place to do that. Take the girl to dinner."

"Yes, sir," Devlin laughed, and watched as the trooper pulled away.

They shared an incredulous look before Devlin put the car into gear and they carefully pulled back into traffic.

"That was too close for comfort," Amberly breathed. "We need to get going anyway. Next big box store you see, stop. I need a burner phone. Or three."

10

Devlin was still shaking his head as he pulled into a local Wal-Mart for Amberly to run in and get a prepaid phone. She'd been dying to call in for the past two days, and he didn't really blame her. If she thought there was someone at the agency or in her group she thought she could trust, he would have to trust her judgement.

It had been gratifying finally getting all that shit off his chest. But now it left him with a new problem. She'd been into the kiss, but only because he'd finally defended himself and given her a story she could believe.

Why hadn't she believed in him without the story?

He understood she was the type that needed proof for everything, but sometimes there needed to be faith in a relationship.

When she returned from the store, she had a bag in hand. Quickly she powered up one of the phones and inserted the sim card, then charged the minutes.

"You know, as soon as you call in, they're tracking you," Devlin warned.

"I know. That's why I'm calling Deputy Director Brown's cell phone. It'll take them a little longer to find me. And if he's dirty, I want a record of his phone activity right now."

Dev grinned at her. "Smart."

Obviously, she had the number memorized, because she punched it in like she'd done it many times before. It rang twice before it was picked up. She punched the button for the speakerphone.

"Brown," a man snapped on the other end.

"It's Temple."

She paused there to get his reaction.

"Where the fuck have you been?" The man exploded, rather dramatically, Dev thought. "This was supposed to be an easy CI meet and I'm somehow cleaning up bodies."

"Yeah," Amberly drawled. "Bodies with CIA identification. Why were they trying to take me out, Brown?"

There was a long pause on the other end of the line. "Are you serious? They weren't CIA. One I ran came back to Georgia Department of Corrections, and the other I'm still looking for. These weren't our guys. Who is the man you're with? I know he's not your CI. We found him dead in the restaurant."

Amberly rolled her eyes toward him, mouth working. "He's a witness. How do I know you're telling me the truth, Brown? I've got people after me."

He paused again, and sighed, which surprised her. It seemed like Brown's mouth was always running and he never showed weakness. "I don't know, honestly, so I'm going to tell you to keep going with what you're doing. I assume you're on Tango II's trail."

"Yes."

"Who did you tell you were going to Chicago?"

"Only the people in my group."

"Okay. I'll be starting my own investigation. If anything timely happens, I need to be apprised."

"Agreed."

And she hung up.

"That was interesting," he said, finally.

"Very," she murmured, looking out over the parking lot. "Let's get a sandwich and a drink at the drive-thru, and we'll get back on the road."

As they pulled through the other side, Amberly tossed the burner phone into the trash receptacle.

They ate their food heading north on I-25 toward Sheridan, Wyoming. They were several hours out, but would be there by the afternoon. The miles sped by, but they talked little. It felt like they were each a little shell-shocked as their worlds recalibrated. Devlin was okay with that. They each had to get used to their new reality. A lot of emotional shit had gone down, and they had to deal with it their own way.

Then she reached over and grabbed his hand, letting them rest clasped on his thigh. His throat closed up, because this was how they'd gone everywhere together, hand in hand.

What an emotional minefield this was.

Wyoming was beautiful and desolate. It was the true wild west, and he wished he had more time to explore. Maybe after they were done saving the country, he thought with a snort.

They arrived in Sheridan in the afternoon, and immediately drove to the address on file for Zed's mother, Carolyn. There were several cars parked in front of the single-story house, and a good bit of activity. It was in a higher end neighborhood, with later model vehicles and people walking their dogs on the sidewalk. There was a small, dusty park across the street and down the block a little, so they parked there to watch the house.

"I might go for a walk," Amberly said. "I need to stretch my legs."

"I'll go with you," he said quickly. It would do them both good to get out. And they could keep the car in sight the entire time.

A path meandered through and circled the shaded park. It wasn't very big. Kids played on the swing sets, squealing and yelling, burning off energy after school. There were a few moms on benches, rocking strollers with one hand and drinking expensive coffees with the other. It was afternoon in Wyoming, so definitely warm, but there were hints that fall would come soon. Some of the leaves were changing on the trees, and the sun was already heading toward the horizon. It was cool enough they didn't stand out wearing their jackets.

A young woman came out of the house they were watching and headed to a blue four-door car in the driveway. She was talking on her phone and never even paused as she drove away. "I think that was Zed's daughter," Amberly murmured. "His mother is disabled, so she's home most of the time. The girl helps take care of her."

Devlin nodded, taking her elbow in his hand to take another loop around the park. "Do we know for sure that he's staying here?"

"No," she huffed. "It's just a guess, because he got out of prison a couple of months ago."

"Well, isn't that fortuitous," he snorted. "Regent gets free as well as one of his boom boom buddies. Any chance that was a coincidence?"

Amberly looked at him sharply. "What are you saying, Devlin?"

"Well, I'm just thinking Regent is getting a lot of help from somewhere..."

She stared at him for a long moment, before turning to look out over the park. "I'm afraid to even consider..."

"But you need to, for your own safety."

"I know."

They stood beneath an oak tree and watched as the teenage girl returned, still talking on her phone, and carried a jug of milk into the house. Devlin glanced at his watch. It was half-past six.

"Dinner time?" he suggested.

"Maybe," she agreed. "Think one of the other vehicles belongs to Zed?"

"Belongs? Maybe not if he just got out of the pen. He might be borrowing one of them."

They watched the house for another forty minutes until the sun sank below the horizon. The park emptied behind them, leaving a few skateboarders taking advantage of the evening.

The front door opened and even from their vantage point, Devlin could see it was the guy they were looking for. Tall and lean, with a thatch of gray hair in a low ponytail on his neck, Zed looked more like a biker than anything. Ragged jeans flapped at his knees and a chain looped around to his wallet. As they watched, he jammed a red ball-cap on his head and pulled a jean-jacket on over his white-ish T-shirt. He stepped down off the porch and followed the sidewalk to the teenage girl's car. Before he could hop in, the girl stepped out onto the porch.

"Don't wreck it," she called.

"I won't, baby," Zed called, and disappeared from view.

Devlin had already turned her toward the Charger. "Let's see where he goes."

They hopped into the car and sped from the park, easily catching up to Zed. He was driving the exact speed limit and using his blinkers more than normal. Devlin allowed a few cars to get in front of him, and followed along at a snail's pace as they headed out the west end of town. Eventually, the other cars either turned off or passed Zed's car.

"He doesn't want to get pulled over," Devlin laughed. "So, he's doing everything he can to be good." Then he pulled into a bar a few miles outside city limits, making Dev chuckle. "Well, not that good, apparently."

Dev continued past the bar, then pulled into the next parking lot and turned around. "We'll wait here a few minutes, then we'll go in and see who he's hanging with. If we're lucky, we'll spot another one of Regent's associates."

"True," Amberly murmured, watching the bar.

They watched people enter and leave for the better part of forty minutes. Then Dev started the car and pulled into the lot. "Do you want to approach him?"

Amberly pursed her lips. "Let's play it by ear and see how things unfold."

"Okay. Do you have cash? I'm about tapped out."

She grinned and nodded. "I have enough for a few beers and some food."

The bar was not overly smoky when they entered, which Dev appreciated. There were booths along the right wall, tables in the middle and the long oak bar was on the left. It was the fullest, with about ten men sitting along the expanse. Zed, their target, sat kind of in the middle on a lone bar stool. No one crowded around him or even talked to him, and he was nursing what looked to be a Coke. Devlin settled at a table a few feet away, but not directly behind him. It wouldn't do to spook the bad guy. Overhead, country music played old classics.

Zed peered around at them, and seemed to survey them for a moment. When Amberly lifted her brows at him, he made a motion with his hand. "Sorry, thought you were someone else."

He turned back around on the stool and didn't look their way again.

A waitress came around and took their drink order, and they ordered some appetizers as well. Then they sat and chatted about mindless stuff, keeping half an ear on the man behind them. Nothing happened for a long time, he just sat drinking his Coke. Then, about halfway through eating their apps, Zed got a phone call.

The ring tone was so loud even over the chatter of the bar, everyone looked around at him, then went back to their own conversations. Dev wanted to lean in and listen hard, but he needn't have worried.

"Yeah, Cole."

A shiver went through him at the sound of the man's name who had haunted him for years. He flashed a look at Amberly, and she very deliberately looked down at the plate of food in front of her. The message was obvious; don't be too eager. Chuckling, Dev nodded at her, but his hunter's instincts had been sparked. He tossed back a swallow of beer, then looked for the server to order another. It gave him a reason to look at the man he might have to kill. Very soon.

"They're not here yet. I don't know what to tell you." Zed huffed out a breath. "Yes, I'm on time. Obviously. Can you hear the buzz of the bar around me? I even got here early."

Zed sat back on the stool, eyes raised to the heavens, as he listened to the man on the other end of the line. Dev wished to high hell he could reach through that phone line and strangle Cole Regent. It would make all of their lives easier.

"Did you tell them the right bar?" Zed glanced around surreptitiously. "I don't see anyone like that. I'm telling you they're not here," he snapped.

Seconds later, he went a little pale and he hunched over the phone. "I'm sorry, Cole. My nerves are shot right now. My daughter is driving me crazy. You'd think she would be happy to see her pop after he's been in prison so long, but all she does is bitch..." He paused for a moment. "God, no! Please, don't! I didn't mean that at all," he hissed.

Zed flagged down the bartender and the man brought him a bottle of whiskey. Zed splashed some into the Coke glass and tossed it back, then he sat there listening to the phone. Dev could see the frustration building in the bouncing knee, and the hunched way he sat. It looked like Cole Regent was chewing his ass good.

"I know you're on a timeline, but I can't make these fuckers appear out of thin air," Zed finally almost yelled. Again, most of the people in the bar glanced at him, and Zed flipped the room the bird. Then he leaned tighter into the phone. For a few seconds Dev lost the conversation as the noise swelled around him, then there was a pause, and he distinctly heard him say, "I know everything rides on this, Cole, but it may be too big this time. I've been with you for a lot of shit, but this one is something else."

A few beats of silence as Zed listened, then he shook his head. "I'm not saying that, damn it. I believe in our calling, too, but I don't think this will translate the way you want it to. Women and children have nothing to do with the laws you're fighting."

Zed huffed out a breath and took another swig of his drink. "Yes, I have the list. I'll call you as soon as they show up."

Dev shared a look with Amberly. If they could get their hands on that list...

Zed pushed a button on the phone and set it very deliberately onto the bar.

"I'm gonna go to the little girl's room, Babe," Amberly said, pushing to her feet. "Whoo," she trilled, giggling as she swayed on her feet.

Dev had watched her nurse her beer and he knew she wasn't as inebriated as she acted. She was just a good actress. Bracing her hand on Dev's shoulder, she reached out her other hand and brushed it across Zed's shoulders. He turned, obviously aggravated, and Amberly grinned at him. "Sorry, dear. Guess I should have eaten a while ago," she breathed, and Zed's expression softened. He gave her a lopsided smile in return, watching as she headed toward the back of the room and the obvious restroom sign.

"Sorry about that," Dev said, getting a good look at the man's face for the first time. Zed wasn't as old as he appeared from a distance. The stringy gray hair and leanness of his body attested to hard times. Dev knew even decent prisons were hard on a man, and if Zed had been in one of the worse ones... well, there was probably a reason why it looked like he'd aged prematurely. "She's such a lightweight."

They chuckled together, and looked back the hallway where she'd disappeared.

"Well," Zed said, "when they're that cute, you pretty much let them do what they want, and just enjoy the ride."

"Isn't that the truth?" Dev laughed again and nodded, turning back to his beer.

Zed turned around to pick up his whiskey.

11

A mberly took the chance to go pee and scrub her hands. It was hard to tell what kind of germs she was touching in here. The front of the house wasn't bad, but this bathroom hadn't seen a good cleaning in ever, maybe. Glancing at the mirror, she grimaced and ran her fingers through her hair, tucking it back, then ran a hand down her nape. It was getting longer here, too. Maybe someday she could think about a haircut...

If she wobbled her way back, maybe she could bump into Zed again. Who the hell was he waiting on?

The CIA had files on Regent back to the early nineties, when he was a troubled kid in an abusive household and all the guns he wanted to play with. His father had been a part of the Militia of Montana, a group built on conspiracy theories and manipulated truths. They wanted to fight the perceived governmental attempt to seize their firearms. They also wanted to stop the country from interfering with their freedoms. Regent's father had eventually gone to prison for a multitude of firearms violations, and had died there of cancer.

Regent had continued on with his father's teachings, landing himself in hot water many times. His vision had been larger than his father's, though, and he'd started building explosive devices, which culminated in his attack on a group protesting automatic rifle sales.

For the most part, that growth and movement of Regent's group was covered by the FBI and later, Homeland Security. The CIA got involved when large transactions of money supporting Regent had been traced out of country, specifically to Russia, then had solidified their involvement when Regent retweeted a Russian Politician's tweet about being in bed with the National Rifle Association, an association Regent had both criticized and praised throughout the years. The NRA had publicly disavowed Regent and his 'radicalized' actions, though the FBI had found connections between the two groups.

The CIA had tried to track Regent down through his tweets, but it was like nailing jello to a wall.

When Regent had blown himself up the first time and gotten caught before he could take out his target, many of the components of the bomb itself had been Russian made. Was he still using the same parts, she wondered.

Stepping out of the bathroom, she put a sway in her hips and a smile on her face. She waved at the bartender for another beer, leaning in to grab it between a couple of men. They glanced at her and smiled, and she sauntered away, back to the table, beer in hand. Zed was in the same position, hunched over his whiskey Coke. She brushed his chair, but didn't try to find the note or anything. Running her hand along Devlin's broad shoulders, she sank into her chair and clunked the beer down. "Hey, baby," she said, grinning at him.

Devlin grinned back at her. And it was a fun moment.

Staking out a current bad guy with a former bad guy. Tipping the beer back, she took a healthy swallow, then grabbed a cold fry, dragging it through a puddle of ketchup. "So, what did you do for three years," she murmured.

Devlin's whiskey-colored eyes flicked to Zed, then back to her. "Well, I took some time off to wrap my head around what had happened, then I started looking for a job. I got on with a contractor who took a chance on me and sent me to school. Then, a few months ago, I broke away from him to create my own company."

Her brows lifted in surprise. "That's incredible. I wondered." She paused. "Did you ever... meet anyone?" she asked, voice hesitant.

Amberly was as surprised as he was that the question had popped out of her mouth. A slow smile crept over his lips. "I did. She's... younger, and blond. Not my normal type at all. She's very obedient."

Her mouth dropped open at him, referring to his girlfriend as obedient. "What the hell?"

Then she saw the glint of laughter in his whiskey eyes and she knew he was messing with her. Pulling out his phone, he scrolled through the pictures. "This is Tink."

She stared at the picture of the running dog incredulously. "Golden retriever?"

Devlin nodded, grinning like a proud papa, and her heart clutched in her chest. He would have been a fantastic dad. "No real girlfriends?" she persisted.

Dev gave her an odd look before finally shaking his head.

She clamped her mouth shut before she asked him about his sexual partners, a little hurt that he would be with anyone, either short or long-term. In her mind, she knew he had probably *been* with someone. Three years was a long time for a man to go without sex, and Devlin had a very high sex drive. At the very least, he had to have an out-of-town hookup, or something.

Why was she thinking about his sex life? It was already hard enough to be with him. Thoughts of how happy they had been before were crowding into her brain, taking her focus from what they needed to be doing, which was catching a killer.

They had wanted a Golden.

A man and a woman walked in. Amberly glanced up, then couldn't seem to glance away. The man was huge, well over six feet tall, dark-haired and square jawed. The guy would be a killer to fight. The woman walking at his side was striking, with long auburn red hair, pale skin and night-dark eyes. She strode into the room as if she could kill, too, lithe and collected even in four-inch heels. They both seemed to focus on Zed at the same time, and Amberly turned around. Her gaze hit Devlin's, and he gave her a cock-eyed smile, then a subtle wink.

At first glance, Zed seemed to be a little out of his depth with the two people that walked in. Amberly would take bets on them being Russian. The male, especially, looked over everything, chin up, like he owned it. And if anyone argued, he would be more than happy to beat them into submission.

The woman chose a stool a little way away from Zed, perching on it carefully. She ran a hand down her thigh, smoothing the fabric of her pants. "I'll have a Cosmopolitan, please," the woman said to the bartender in heavily accented English.

"Beer," the big man said. "The biggest you have."

The bartender, a guy in his thirties, tipped an imaginary cap at them. "Coming right up."

"I guess we have stereotypes for a reason," Devlin murmured, and Amberly laughed.

It was so hard to look at Devlin and talk about innocuous things, when ninety percent of her focus was on the Russian couple. She no longer felt the pain in her arm or the tiredness in her bones. All the worry about the corrupt agents faded away as she did her best not to just turn around and watch the newcomers, because she knew some kind of deal was about to go down.

Through the speakers positioned around the bar, a slow dance began to play, and in one corner of her brain she recognized it as one that she and Devlin had danced to the night they got married. Before she could decline, Devlin pulled her to her feet and onto the dance floor.

"What the hell are you doing?" she hissed, truly angry but really trying not to show it on her face.

Devlin grinned down at her. "Oh, honey, you know this is one of our songs," he said plaintively, and a little louder than necessary.

Amberly glanced around. They were not the only couple dancing, at least, but she wasn't going to let him off the hook. "Why did you drag me out here?"

Devlin pulled her tight and moved into an easy, swaying dance. "Because I specifically remember dancing to this on our honeymoon in Aruba. And the night we got married. Do you remember?"

"Yes," she admitted grudgingly, "but this isn't the time or place to dance down memory lane. The players are here. We need to be listening and gathering as much intel as we can."

"Granted," he murmured, "but we also need to look like a believable couple. We have history. Why not let them see that?"

She shook her head with a huff, and he reached up to

brush her dark bangs away from her forehead. "Besides," he whispered, "They haven't even connected yet. It'll be a few minutes before they get down to business."

Amberly knew he was right. She just hated to admit it.

"Just give yourself a minute to remember. Then we'll sit down and be superspies, listening to the Russians make a deal with a paramilitary flunky."

Amberly snorted. "Fine, but no grabbing my ass."

"Oh, baby, that was the best part," Devlin growled in her ear, sending shivers up her spine. Then he slid his hands low on her hips and spread his fingers wide, aligning their bodies.

Amberly breathed out a sigh and rested her head on his chest. She could feel how excited he was to have her in his arms. "Oh, Devlin."

For just a moment, she would allow herself to be just Amberly, a woman once in love with a dangerous man. They swayed across the dance floor, reacquainting themselves with each other, and she knew it was a dangerous thing, being with him like this. Because it would make her want again, and she didn't know if she could survive it if it fell through.

They swayed and brushed and teased, and when the music ended, they stared at one another for a long moment, before quicker, upbeat music chased them from the floor. They walked back to the table, hand in hand, and she didn't want it to be because they were undercover. She wanted him to hold her hand because he wanted to, not because of some obligation.

And there was no way of knowing what they were walking into going after Regent. Maybe she should snatch at the happiness she could. Last night she'd held back, but if he approached her the same way tonight, there would be no turning away.

They settled into their chairs and Amberly shifted hers over a little, so that she and Devlin could brush shoulders. It's also gave her a little better line of sight to what was going on a few yards away.

The Russians had gotten their drinks and were more than halfway done with them. Even as she watched, the big male tipped his head back and swallowed down the rest of the mug of beer. The bartender brought him another, removing the empty. The couple didn't really seem to be talking to one another, but maybe she just couldn't hear them.

"Hopefully they'll come to him," she murmured, reaching up to run her fingers under his chin. The bristles were growing in a little. It had been at least a week or two since he'd shaved. She'd always loved the grunge look on him. Two whiter lines of hair bracketed his mouth, his chin still fairly dark. Devlin had had almost black hair most of his life and at one time she thought that was when he'd been most handsome. But seeing him settle into his age was even better.

"We should be so lucky," he said, capturing her hand and kissing her fingers. "How is your arm?"

"It's all right," she said. "I don't want to enter a rowing competition or anything, but it'll work if I need it to."

Within a couple of minutes, Zed motioned to the bartender for another bottle of whiskey. Once he got it, he carried it over to sit on the other side of the Russian female. Outside of their range of hearing.

"Shit," she murmured. There was no way they would hear anything that far away.

"Don't worry about it. It'll work out," Devlin said quietly.

Amberly didn't think so. When she'd left for the meet in Chicago, she hadn't planned on going any further than Chicago and the single meeting, so she didn't have a lot of the fun toys the CIA had available to their officers. What she wouldn't give for a damn bug right this minute. Even if it looked awkward as hell, she'd get it over there somehow. But, it wasn't gonna happen.

Frustration boiled in her and it was hard to remember that she couldn't just go over there and hold them at gunpoint to make them tell her what they knew.

"We just have to be patient," he told her calmly.

Amberly could only see what they were missing out on. Vital information was being shared there, and she couldn't get to it. "Maybe I can go compliment the woman or something," she whispered.

"Don't worry about it," he told her calmly. "Give it a few minutes."

And he was right. Within about five minutes, things began to happen. The big Russian jerked his head around at something Zed said, then the woman rocked her head back and laughed, drawing the gazes of most of the men in the bar. The woman slid off the stool, saying, "You two work it out. I have to find restroom."

In her tall heels, she swayed through the bar. It was obvious she loved the male attention, and she did the most with the body she had. Amberly moved to follow her, but Devlin put a hand on her arm. "Too obvious. Just wait."

Amberly gnashed her teeth, aggravated that he wasn't allowing her to do her job.

"If you follow her, she's going to know you're some flavor of government. I'm telling you, stay put."

Amberly forced a smile, even as she planned how to kick Devlin in the balls while sitting down.

Zed and the other man weren't getting along well, either, it didn't seem like. Their faces were tense, and their body language was stilted. The woman had left them to iron things out and they appeared to be getting worse. She looked at Devlin and glimpsed the red-haired woman over Devlin's shoulder. She was staring straight at Amberly, as if she was aware that Amberly had been paying too much attention to their conversation.

The woman stopped beside Devlin's shoulder, propping a hand on one curvy hip. "Aren't you two a cute couple," she purred.

Devlin rocked back in his chair to look up at her and grinned. "Thank you, ma'am. I think she's the cute half, though."

Amberly grimaced. "Whatever," she said slowly, exaggerating her slur a little. She leaned toward the woman a little. "Is there going to be a fight? It doesn't seem like they're getting along."

The woman waved an elegant hand, tipped with bright red fingernails. "They will be fine. Just working out the bill."

"I told my..." Amberly stuttered to a halt, her tongue tangling. "My...ex, friend, Dev, that I didn't want to get in the middle of anything."

"My ex friend Dev?" the woman repeated, eyes sharp on Amberly's face.

Incredibly, color suffused her face. This should be an easy interaction, but for some reason her mouth wasn't working.

"We haven't seen each other for a few years," Devlin interjected smoothly, drawing the woman's attention back to him. "She's my ex-wife, but things might be warming up," he said, grinning as he covered her hand with his own. Amberly felt heat creeping through her cheeks again.

"Stop it, damn it," she hissed.

The woman tipped her head back and laughed. "You both are twice the fool," she said, shaking her head as she walked away.

Amberly looked at Devlin as the woman walked away. "Thank you," she mouthed.

His only response was a wink.

12

Dev hoped he'd played off Amberly's stumble well enough. He thought he had, but the woman was sharp. Even after she moved back to Zed and the man she'd entered with, she still glanced at their table occasionally. Dev thought she was checking for actual affection, so he made sure to hang onto Amberly's hand, and when a slow dance came up he dragged her onto the floor.

Amberly protested, of course, but Dev whispered into her ear that they were being watched. Thoroughly. And that she needed to keep up the ruse. After that, they danced a little closer, and she made sure to stare into his eyes more.

Dev was thoroughly hooked all over again. Amberly had been fun when they'd been dating, and he could still remember how impressed he'd been with her. Yeah, she'd been wearing a stunning midnight blue cocktail dress at the time, but he remembered thinking that she was the most beautiful, dangerous woman he'd ever met, and he was intrigued. She still struck him that way, which was a good thing because she absolutely loved fighting for her country.

It was so odd, because he'd been given the perfect

excuse he needed to do exactly what he wanted to do, hang on her every word and touch.

They eventually sat down, and he waved at the bartender for another round.

"I don't know if I should," Amberly said.

"We'll nurse these ones. If you want, we can go wait outside until the meeting is done."

She gave him a scathing look. "Not even, buddy."

Dev chuckled. There was no chance she would have taken him up on that offer. They settled back, nursing their drinks, and even though they were supposed to be working, he was having fun.

And then the Russians got mad.

The woman stood up first, glaring at Zed, and she made some kind of motion with her hands they couldn't see, because her back was to them. Zed put his hands out, palms up, like he was saying 'what do you expect me to do?'. The woman leaned in, finger pointed at his face, and whispered something furiously. Then she laid him out with a single, beautiful round house punch.

Zed smashed through stools and went down like a sack of potatoes, stunned. The woman stepped over him, muttered something in Russian and headed toward the door. The man with her looked down at Zed and shook his head, spat on him, and followed after the woman.

Dev and Amberly were both on their feet and moving to 'help' Zed. Amberly reached him first, kneeling down to help him sit up. Dev saw her pocket the shopping list as he reached a hand down to help Zed to his feet. The man was rubbing his jaw, but there was desolation in his eyes. Dev thought he might have even seen tears.

Dev motioned for the people that had crowded around to back off.

"Are you okay, buddy? She really walloped you."

The man shook his head, looking down at the floor. "He's going to kill me. He's going to kill me."

Dev jiggled his arm. "What are you talking about? Who's going to kill you?"

"Cole," Zed said shortly, shaking his head. "I'm fucked. I'm fucked," he whispered.

Zed's cell-phone beeped with an incoming message, and he jumped, pulling it from his pocket. His hard face seemed to crumple, and Dev saw the message.

2 mins to respond or i call your kid.

Zed backed out of screens and found a phone number. He pressed the green call button and listened to it ring, ring, ring... then a voice picked up, but it was voicemail. Zed immediately called the number again. Same results. Desperate, his hands shaking, he got into the text mode and typed out a message. *Put phone int he yard! Right now! ill explain later!!!*

"Are you okay, dude?" Dev asked him, trying to be solicitous.

"I'm fine," Zed snapped, shaking his arm free. "Fuck off."

He moved a few feet away, obviously going through the call screen again and trying to call his daughter. When there was no response, his face crumpled in fear. They were close enough to see him get into the text screen. His thumb hesitated over a button for several long seconds, then he hit it.

Dev turned to Amberly. "Give me a hundred bucks."

"What?"

"Just give me a hundred dollar bill."

Scowling, she dug in her pocket for the money, and handed it over. "You'd better know what you're doing because I don't have a lot of cash left."

Dev turned and slid the hundred dollar bill and a stack

of twenties across the bar to the bartender. The man grinned, winked, and slid a phone back across. Dev pocketed the phone without looking at it. Then reached back across and shook the man's hand. It had been fortuitous to find a fellow former Navy man.

Zed was walking out the door, head down, phone to his ear. They followed along behind, but back a little. They could have been right behind the man, and he probably wouldn't have noticed because he was pleading with Cole on the other end.

"Do you think the daughter is in danger?" Amberly whispered.

"Definitely. The message he sent her said put the phone in the yard. It seems like an incredibly small explosive device, but if they have it to their ear, I suppose it wouldn't have to be big."

"That's horrific."

They watched Zed cross the lot to his daughter's blue car, still talking on the phone. The parking lot lights had come on, sending out weak light, but it was easy enough to see Zed lean against the side of the car. The conversation was mostly quiet, but at one point he burst out, "There was nothing I could do!"

Then they heard him apologize profusely for yelling. There was a beat of silence, then Zed started to plead. "Please, Cole, don't do this. We've known each other a long time and you know I'll back any play you make, but you can't hurt my daughter. The Russians didn't want to deal for the money we offered them. I can't do anything about that."

Dev pulled out his phone and found Charley's number. He typed off a quick text and added Zed's address as well as their own. He didn't know if anything could be done, but he would try. An innocent teenage girl had no business dying for her father's misdeeds.

Then he paged through his phone to find the recording app. He pulled up the last recording, taken nine minutes ago, and hit the white play button on the app. Glancing around the parking lot, he made sure it was quiet, other than Zed pleading a dozen cars away, and he shaded the light of the phone with his hand.

"We have everything you need on your list," the woman said, her voice heavily accented and tinny from the app. "But the price has gone up. Three million."

"What," Zed hissed. "You said two million four days ago. That's what I have available."

"Yes, but that was before your boss started drawing attention to himself. He's supposed to be dead, yet, here you are. There is blood in the water, and we are taking a risk by even talking to you."

"No one knows what he's doing yet," Zed argued.

"That's not what we heard. There was a meet in Chicago with an informant from your camp."

"What? Who?"

"That we don't know. But it was messy. Now the CIA is looking at us again."

"That's not my problem. Just because you're getting greedy..."

That was when the punch happened and the noise went crazy. Dev hit the pause button and put the phone away.

"So, what are we doing?" Amberly hissed, leaning close.

"Obviously, Zed is important to Cole. Zed probably knows exactly where Cole is and what he's planning. If we could interrogate him, and then stash him somewhere..."

"I can call Brown, see if he can send a team."

Dev looked at Amberly, and he saw the reservation in her expression. Even she knew that was a reach.

Dev shrugged. "If they know they have a high-value target coming in, it might flush out the ones trying to cover everything up. Somebody has an agenda that agrees with Cole's. "

She nodded, looking worried. "Let's get what we can out of him."

They turned toward Zed, who was still pleading with Cole. It was pretty humiliating to listen to. Guns in hand, they crouched and began to move in.

That was when the plan went to hell. Out of the darkness, a car revved and tires squealed. Dev thought they were the targets, but when the car suddenly flipped on its lights, he realized Zed was the target. It had to be the Russians. Then they heard the subtle *thwop thwop* of a silenced weapon. Both of Zed's arms flung out as he flew back, into the gravel of the lot and disappeared behind a car.

Bracing his own weapon on the top of a truck bed, Dev focused on the flash of taillights as the driver spun the wheel and gassed it through the lot. It wasn't his rifle, but the Beretta did the job. He heard the bullets hit the car, and he thought he might have heard someone cry out. Had he gotten the driver?

Dev was racing after the car before he even realized what he was doing, firing constantly, and when the mag emptied, he slammed in the second one. The headlights of the car spun wildly before it slammed into the ass end of a pick-up truck, where it stopped. Dev crouched, using cover to get close to the vehicle. He could hear the man's accented voice, pleading with someone to get up. "Alina, baby, get up. Alina."

Dev crept forward, and even from ten feet away, he could

see that the woman with the beautiful red hair would not be waking again. The man seemed to recognize this at the same time, because he looked up with fury in his eyes. When he saw Dev standing in front of the car, he immediately lifted a weapon from the seat and fired.

The closest cover was the Russian's car, so he dove down in front of the car's front bumper. The Russian continued to fire until the weapon clicked empty, then Dev heard him push the door open.

Fuck... he did not want to have to fight the over-muscled thug. Rolling, he looked beneath the car for the man's feet, and fired. Crying out, the big man stumbled, but he still managed to reach Dev. With a lunging punch, the guy damn near knocked him out. Dev still had hold of his weapon, though. Angling it up, he pulled the trigger. Then pulled it again and again, until the massive Russian stopped moving.

Shoving his body to the side, Dev allowed himself to breathe for a moment, before sitting up. The world tilted crazily and he gagged, wondering if the fucker had given him a concussion with that single punch. Sparkles spun around him, and he dragged in oxygen.

Amberly was calling for him. He could hear her and he knew he needed to get up.

"Come on, asshole," he muttered. "Get moving!"

Bracing a hand on the car's front bumper, he shoved to his feet. Then he had to stand there a minute as the world settled around him. He was nauseated as fuck, but he moved his feet.

Amberly had to be okay.

13

Z ed was dying.

There was a bullet hole through his right upper chest that was fatal. This far out of town, there would be no squad to save him. At this point, he would need to have a surgeon inside the bar with an equipped operating room in the back in order to live.

The man's eyes were a startling shade of bright green, something she hadn't noticed before, and they were frantic. "You have to check my daughter. She doesn't know anything about what's going on. Please," he gurgled, blood flowing from his mouth.

"What does Cole have planned, Zed? Help me save lives."

"Help my daughter," he pleaded.

"Tell me what he has planned and I'll save a bunch of daughters. And yours as well. I promise."

Zed dragged in a breath, and it looked difficult. "He's got these ideas," he said, wheezing.

"What are his targets, Zed?"

"Ri-Riverview Preparatory school, the Academy of the

Holy Cross, the Martin Luther King Jr. Library, and more I can't remember. Children and women. It's wrong. There's a maternity building."

The man blinked, staring straight up at the sky, and Amberly knew she was running out of time. "Are there explosive devices in the phones?"

Zed nodded. "Just some of us got them. And he made us give them to our family. Leverage."

"Who is the little girl at the school in Fort Collins?"

Rocking his head from side to side on the gravel, he grimaced in pain.

"Devlin!" she screamed, praying he was okay. This information was too important to leave. The country could literally depend upon this man's dying words.

"Zed, who is the little girl?" she demanded.

His hand had fallen to his side, and she didn't know what to do for him. "I'll help your daughter," she promised.

His eyes flickered. "The girl is the granddaughter of his contact at the CIA, the one that got us out... He wanted leverage, just in case..."

Zed's hand lifted and he handed her his phone. "One one six four."

Those green, green eyes closed for the last time and his hand fell away, the cell phone skittering in the gravel. She checked his carotid to be sure and there was no more beat.

"Fuck..." Amberly breathed, sitting back on her heels, then reached out to snatch up the phone. She didn't have time to mope or look at it, because Devlin was out there in the night somewhere.

Pushing to her feet, she shoved the phone in her pocket and took off running toward where she'd heard the last gunshots. People were peering out of the bar. "Someone call 911," she yelled.

Gun in hand, she pushed on, looking and listening for any sounds of fighting or altercation. She didn't hear anything. "Devlin?"

"Here," she heard, and rounded the front corner of a van. Dev was leaning against the quarter panel, looking dazed. Blood covered him at the midsection, but when she started digging at his shirt, he pushed her away. "It's not mine," he told her. "It's his. I think I'm fine, other than a knock to the head."

Gripping his chin in her hand, she looked up into his dazed eyes. "Are you okay?"

"Yeah, my balance is shit, though. He seriously rung my bell."

Hoisting his arm over her shoulders, Amberly led him back across the lot to their car. Zed's body lay where he'd died, and she thought she could hear sirens way in the distance. She wasn't going to stick around to find out. Digging in Devlin's hip pocket, she found the key fob and unlocked the car. She guided Devlin to the passenger side and dropped him down into the seat, then stretched the seat belt across his chest. Circling the hood of the car, she climbed into the driver's seat, reaching for her own seatbelt.

She tore out of the lot, tossing Zed's cell phone into the back seat. They needed to look at it and get it the fuck out of the car as soon as possible. She was sure she could get into his Google and track his movements, and hopefully that would tell her exactly where Cole Regent was.

AMBERLY HAD to pull over once to allow Devlin to puke, then they were on the road again. They needed to get to Zed's daughter. Devlin had a concussion, but she doubted he would allow her to take him to a hospital. They had too much to do.

Devlin reached into his pocket and pulled out his cell phone, then started swiping through screens. His eyes were squinted, and she had a feeling he was in a huge amount of pain right now. "How did you get the concussion?"

"That big fucker hit me. One time," he complained. "That's all it took. Not sure if you noticed or not but his fists were damn near twice the size of mine."

Amberly snorted. "Okay..."

Devlin had his head down, reading a text. "Charley says a team has been dispatched to collect Zed's daughter."

"They need the bomb squad or something to dispose of the cell phone," she told him quickly. "It has a small explosive device in it, like we thought. I have Zed's. We need to look at it as soon as possible."

"Well, pull over. This is as good of a place as any."

Yeah, he was right. There was nothing around here, just scrub bushes and sand. There was also a dirt road on the right, so she turned there, then stopped after about a mile and parked at the side of the road, leaving the headlights on to illuminate the area in front of them. Reaching for the phone in the back seat, she climbed out of the car and walked into the scrub a bit. Devlin followed along behind, looking pale and ill. "Are you okay," she asked, genuinely worried.

"I'll be fine," he murmured. "How are you going to get into it?"

Amberly snorted. "He gave me the code before he died."

She keyed it in, opening the phone, and started searching through the history. "It looks like he's been mostly in Sheridan, though there are several trips up to Billings, and it looks like two trips out to a wildlife preserve north-east of Bozeman. I bet that's where Cole is, out there beyond roads and towns."

"He has to be close enough for cell-phone service, though. How else could he carry his threats out?"

"True," she murmured, scanning. "It looks like he stayed in the same place each time he went to Bozeman."

"Give me the address," Devlin said, pulling out his own phone. She read it off and he keyed it in. "Got it. Where else?"

She reeled off a couple of other addresses, then got into his contacts and text messages. Tension constricted her chest, because she knew that this phone could explode in her hands at any moment.

So, when a new text came in, making the phone beep, she might have let out a very un-CIA like scream. Devlin outright laughed at her, then gripped his head in his hands. "That was funny. I bet it's Cole. Open it."

It *was* Cole.

listen to me you son of a bitch, you'd better respond. Your daughter is dead. Are you next?

She realized then there were a line of unanswered texts. "It says his daughter is dead. Should I respond?"

"Yes, tell him... something..."

Amberly paged back through the old messages. Neither one of them were much for grammar. *with the contacts. Give me a minute. Please dont kill my daughter.*

Devlin was texting on his phone. "Charley says the daughter is safe but the phone exploded outside the house before the bomb squad could get there."

Well, at least the daughter was safe.

Amberly paged through the messages, pulling out pertinent details and reading them off to Devlin. He was typing them into texts, she assumed to this mysterious

Charley. Or maybe on a notes app. It was going in writing somewhere.

Zed?

yeah, she typed off.

She found the downloads section and starting looking through it, just in case... Nothing. She went to the camera app and starting looking through pics.

"Oh, get your camera! Video!" she told Devlin quickly.

A picture of a picture on a phone was never perfect, but she couldn't afford to take the time or risk of connection to send it directly to his phone. She started flipping through pictures, pausing just long enough for it to still, then moving on. It looked like Zed had been the one to take the original pictures. Obviously, as soon as he'd gotten out of prison, he'd been sent on errands.

The phone rang in her hand and she gasped. It said Cole.

"We can't answer it. Keep paging through pics."

She did as told and kept flipping. Some of the places were familiar to her and others were not. Anxiety beat at her. "I think he's going to blow it. He has to know something is up."

Devlin continued to record as she flipped, but Amberly felt like she was out of time. With a jostling move, she sent the phone flying. It landed in the dirt about twenty feet away.

Nothing happened.

Devlin gave a raspy chuckle. "I think you were a..."

The blast that struck them was just strong enough to knock them on their asses. Amberly gasped, then choked on dust, coughing. She sat up first, brushing burning debris from her clothes. "What the fuck! That's overkill. No pun."

Devlin moaned, holding his head as he lay in the dirt. Amberly brushed crap off of him, too. "Are you okay, babe?"

"I feel like a roadside bomb just went off beneath me."

He rolled to his side and retched. Amberly frowned. That was one of the signs of a serious concussion. "Well, it was kind of a roadside bomb. It was beside the road, anyway."

She looked at the remnants of the phone. It had blown a hole in the dirt about five feet across, and flattened the straggly grass for another twenty feet around. The grass nearest the center was burning. She would need to stomp that out before they left.

"Fuck," she hissed, scraping her hair back.

Wrapping her arms around his shoulders, she helped him to his feet. Then she held onto him, because he had a definite sway. Devlin wrapped his arms around her shoulders and braced his head on top of hers. "Hold still just a minute, please," he said softly.

Amberly held him. Actually, she kind of sagged into him. Or they sagged into each other. What a fucking unbelievable night. Tiredness beat at her, but excitement too. They now had more information than they ever had, and she wanted to move on it. Their bodies were not keeping up with their determination, though. They needed sleep and food, and maybe a damn shower. And she still had only dirty clothes to put on.

For just a moment, the task of what lay before them hit her. The entire country was depending upon them, and she needed to go to the bathroom.

14

D ev's phone survived the blast, though it did have a few new scratches across the screen. He'd tried to watch the video, but his head was reeling. If he could get some solid mattress time, he would probably be okay, but they really needed to stop and take a breath. After all the traveling they'd done, the stakeout of Zed's house, the bar scene, killing the Russians, and almost being killed themselves, they needed to take a breath.

Amberly was driving, and she didn't look a lot better than he did. Her dark hair was a straggly mess across her forehead, and there was a bruised look around her eyes. It hadn't been an easy day mentally, either.

The car began to slow and he cracked his eyes open. They were pulling into a quaint little motel, conveniently located next to a small, beat down strip mall. "Bed," he nodded, "food, a discount store, and laundry. You couldn't have done any better, babe."

Amberly gave him a tired smile as she pulled into the lot. "Right?"

Dev watched as she went into the office of the motel. He

wondered how much cash she had, because he didn't have much either. As a last resort, he could probably use his bank card, but it would be a glaring red flag to anyone looking. They should probably lose the car, soon, as well.

Maybe after he'd had a chance to sleep. Closing his eyes, he waited for Amberly to come out of the office.

He woke to tapping on the glass by his head, and she waved a key.

The room was on the ground floor and was spotlessly clean. "Wow," Amberly breathed, walking in and dropping her dirty bag to the floor. "I don't even want to touch anything until I get a shower."

"Go ahead," he said. "I'll secure the door and look at the video for a few minutes."

Indecision crossed her face. "Actually, I'm going to run to the discount store for something clean to wear, then get my clothes into a washer. I'm sick of being grimy, and this clean room really makes me want to be clean."

He snorted. "Okay. Do what you need to do. I think we're fairly safe here."

"No one followed us that I saw. When I come back from the store, I'll park the car around back. We're going to need to change it out. Do you have laundry you want done?"

"I'll grab it. Yeah, I know," he said softly, digging into his bag. "I'd already decided to go scouting after I get some sleep."

They were still jiving on the same wavelength, all these years later. He handed his clothes off to her and caught her hand before she pulled away. Deliberately, he stepped into her space and leaned down to give her a kiss. "I'm very glad we survived tonight. There isn't anyone I would rather have at my side in a firefight."

Incredibly, her cheeks went pink, and she grinned. "Yeah, you're not too bad yourself, old man."

Dev groaned as he chuckled. "I'm totally feeling my age tonight. Go get your clean on so we can get some sleep. I'll shower while you're gone."

"Okay."

Leaning up, she gave him a quick kiss on the lips, then disappeared with his dirty laundry.

Taking his phone and his weapon into the bathroom with him, Dev stripped down and stepped into the hot running water. Oh, it hurt so good. There was a convenient bench along the back wall, so, adjusting the head, he angled the water to fall over him. He watched the dirty water swirl down the drain, then closed his eyes.

Dev jerked awake as he was tipping forward in sleep. Catching himself, he sighed. Maybe he was tired. Ripping open the fresh soap, he lathered up and rinsed, then stepped out of the stall. Rubbing the towel over his not sore areas, he got mostly dry, and stepped out of the room. Amberly hadn't returned yet, but he'd expected it to take her a while to get things done. Or at least started. He doubted she would sit there and watch the clothes wash.

Tucking his gun beneath his pillow, he rested his spinning head to the soft cloth, pulled the sheet over his damp body and was out almost immediately.

AMBERLY LET herself into the motel room quietly, which was hard to do with the bags she was carrying. Latching the door behind her, she slid the deadbolt home, and set the bags on the two person table by the front window.

After she'd bought her supplies, she'd gone into the

discount store bathroom, done a quick wipe down with baby wipes to get the worst of the blood and dirt off of her, then changed her clothes. She was clean-er at least, as she pulled on the granny panties and gray sweats. All of her clothes were in the dryer now, as well as most of Devlin's. She would go get them in about forty minutes, then have a proper shower before she allowed herself to slow down.

Opening one of the paper bags, she retrieved an aluminum container with a white cardboard lid. The all-night diner hadn't been much to look at, but it had smelled amazing. So, she'd ordered two of the specials. It was lasagna with garlic bread, and as she worked off the lid, she was so glad that she'd gotten it. The scent of garlic was like ambrosia, and she inhaled deeply. Ripping the plastic fork from the wrapper, she dug in, almost inhaling the food. They'd eaten apps at the bar, but they'd expended a huge amount of energy tonight which needed replenished.

Devlin murmured in his sleep, but didn't wake, even over her rustling the plastic. She would give him an hour, then wake him up. If he did have a concussion, he needed to be checked regularly.

The lasagna was delicious, and she felt guilty for eating the entire entree. Whatever. There was one for Devlin, too. She glanced at the clock on the bedside table. She had about ten more minutes before she could go get her clothes. Moving to the side of the bed in front of him, she rested her hand on his arm. "Devlin."

A slow smile spread across his lips as his eyes cracked open, and it was so sweet. "I've missed you waking me. Sometimes when I was falling asleep, I would hear you call my name, and I would jerk awake. I always wondered if you needed me then, and I just wasn't there for you."

Unexpected tears filled her eyes, and she had to blink

them away. She'd had nightmares as well, that he was blaming her for giving up on them. Or that he was being shot, and she turned away and walked into her office. That one was very vivid in her mind. This sweetness was more than she deserved, because she had literally and figuratively walked away from him. "I had similar dreams," she admitted, running her hand up through his hair. His eyes sagged closed again, though the smile stayed.

"I missed you touching me like this," he murmured, so she continued to run her hand through his hair and down his head. She'd checked for knots earlier, and could only find the bruise on his jaw. It was darkening to a deep purple now. "There's food on the table if you want it. I'm going to go get the clothes from the dryer."

"Okay. Be careful, my heart."

And he breathed out, already asleep.

Amberly wiped at her eyes. That was what he had called her when they were in love. My heart.

Moving quickly, she went and retrieved their laundry, bundling it into a bag. She would fold it when she got back. Then she returned to the motel room. Devlin hadn't moved while she was gone. Securing the door with the dead bolt and a chair, she made sure every inch of the window was sealed, then finally moved to the bathroom. She cranked the hot water, almost vibrating with anticipation. The granny panties went in the trash. There was one more pair out in the bag that would be her absolute last alternative. Then she shucked her clothes. Grabbing the little bottle of shampoo and body wash, she stepped beneath the water.

It was almost enough to make her cry. Or maybe she did cry, for everything they'd had to do today. Seeing the phone that had literally just been in her hand blow up was shocking, and a little terrifying. If Regent had given his people, more importantly, their families, these phones, it was a horrible, foolproof way to keep them in line.

But then, Regent was proving himself to be the monster she'd known him to be. The list of targets were all soft targets, meaning schools and places that didn't normally have security.

She needed to call Brown. God, she hoped he wasn't the dirty one.

Wait... the little girl at the school. Zed had said that she was the granddaughter of the CIA contact that had been helping them out. So, the guy had to be in his fifties or sixties. Right? Maybe late forties.

Brown needed to get someone on that kid, a team, preferably. She would probably have one of those phones. If it went off while she was at lunch or in a class, it could take out a dozen kids. Or more, if they were huddled together. The thought made her stomach turn.

With a final rinse, she stepped out of the stall, drying off quickly. If she could get a quick call in to Brown, then she could sleep somewhat peacefully, knowing that she'd at least done something.

Once she was dressed in her tee and black panties, she sat down at the table and glanced at the clock. It didn't matter what time it was. She called Brown. He answered on the first ring.

Amberly heaved a breath. "I need you to answer a question, Brown, and be completely honest."

"This had better be good, Temple."

"Do you have grandkids?"

"Fuck, no!" the man burst out. "You have to have a family to do that first. And I don't have one. What's your point?"

Amberly had to make a judgement call to trust Brown, and she plunged into the story. She didn't tell him about

Devlin yet, but he would probably figure that out on his own in no time. It wasn't going to come from her mouth, though.

She gave Brown the list of targets that Zed had given them, and forwarded the video on to him. "I can't tell you strenuously enough, you need to get a team out to Colorado to track down that girl's parents and figure out who the fuck her granddad is, because that's your corrupt asshole."

"I'm planning the team now. It'll be officers less than forty. What is his big plan?"

"I'm not sure exactly. Zed knew about the targets, but he didn't say anything specific about what was going to happen at those targets. It could be anything. Regent seems to be a bit of a coward, though. I don't think he'll attack them all at once. I think he'll go for the one he screwed up last time personally."

"I think you're right," Brown agreed. "Okay, your task is to figure out where the fuck he is and what he's doing. Feed me intel as you get it. And if you get the chance, take the fucker out. We'll deal with the aftermath later."

"Roger that," she said, and hung up.

Almost immediately, her eyes seemed to droop. It was like her body had given it's all, and was now shutting down, whether she it wanted to or not. Heading into the bathroom, she did a final pee and brushed her teeth, then climbed into the second bed. The sheets felt like butter, and she turned on her side. At the last minute, she set her alarm to check on Devlin in the night, then she closed her eyes.

15

Devlin woke up wanting biscuits and gravy. He settled for cold lasagna, and it was damn good. When you're so hungry your stomach thinks your neck has been cut, you don't get to be picky.

Amberly was still sleeping, which was fine. He could tell by the neatly stacked laundry that she'd been up well past when he'd crashed. Looking around, he could see she'd done a lot last night. Then he caught sight of something familiar.

Peeking from the corner of her backpack was the little beaded elephant bag he'd gotten her years ago from a stall in Turkey. It had been cheap and quirky, but cute. He picked it up, holding it in his hands. Years ago, she'd kept a sonogram picture of the baby they'd almost had. Was it still in here? Would he be invading her privacy to look?

Unable to help himself, he unzipped the bag. In amongst a few makeup products was a laminated sonogram picture. This was what she'd gone back for in Chicago. It was why she'd risked being caught. To collect the only picture of the only baby she'd almost had.

His throat tightened as he looked at her. Maybe if they'd stayed together, they could have tried again... Dev shook off the melancholy and tucked the bag away in her backpack.

Once done with his Italian breakfast, he headed out the door to reconnoiter. The throbbing in his head had mostly gone away, though he felt like he could sleep another eighteen hours. The morning outside was crisp and fresh. It was the kind of morning that encouraged nursing a coffee on a front porch or in bed with the one you loved.

He'd love to go right back into the bedroom and curl up with her.

They had a fugitive to kill, though.

Devlin looked around, checking for cameras or any other kind of security. Nothing. The lights were on in the office, but when he peered through the window, there was an old man asleep tipped back in an old office chair, almost to the point of toppling over. He wouldn't see shit.

So, Dev started scouting vehicles. He wasn't impressed by what he found, though. Yeah, there were a few he could hotwire, but they were beaters not worth his time. One even had the keys hanging from the ignition, almost as if the owner was hoping someone would steal it. Yeah, not today, fuckers.

Dev headed back to the room. They would keep the Charger for now, even though the owner had to have reported it missing by now. Their only advantage was that the iron gray charger was one of thousands, and if he didn't attract attention unnecessarily, they would be fine.

Amberly had kicked the sheets off when he walked in, and he couldn't help but admire her. It was obvious she'd worked hard to get her body to this level, and he was proud of her. She looked up at him and smiled, then launched into a bone cracking stretch.

Dev immediately went hard, because her breasts were perfectly outlined by that thin t-shirt. "Oh, baby, you are absolutely stunning."

"Right," she drawled, turning her head to him, her eyes sleepy.

Dev knew it wasn't the ideal time or place, but he needed to do it. Locking the door behind him, he crossed the room and sank down on the bed beside her hip. Without giving her a chance to protest, he leaned down and took her mouth.

"Mm," she hummed "Good morning. How is your head?"

Dev pulled back to look down at her. "Doesn't hurt a bit right now," and he grinned.

Amberly smacked him on the shoulder, even as she pulled him down for another kiss.

Dev probably would have been okay with a good morning kiss, but then she shifted her hips, lying flat, and angling her thigh out in invitation. Saying no was not a possibility, but he did pull back enough to look down at her. "Babe?"

"Let's not overthink this, Devlin. I want you. You know that. I've never stopped wanting you."

Dev couldn't have asked for anything more. As quickly as he could, he tossed his clothes and settled onto the bed with her. Somehow, she'd gotten her own panties off while he was distracted. Opening her arms, she guided him to nestle between her thighs.

Dev really tried to go slow, but when she met his mouth with her own, her tongue sweeping out to slide against his, he knew neither one of them were going to last long. Lifting her knees, Amberly reached down with one hand and guided him into her.

Dev's throat tightened with emotion as he felt the sweetest homecoming ever, gliding into her body. They'd said it to each other many times over the years. The house was not the home. Home was the person inside the house. And home was finding the person that matched you perfectly, who was your counterpoint.

As he slid into her, it literally felt like he had found his other half. Again. He'd found her once and lost her. But he wasn't going to lose her again. The sense of familiarity and peace he felt was more important to him than the orgasm rolling his way.

"Oh," she breathed, her hands coming up to cup his face. "I've missed you."

His hips flexed spasmodically, surging into her again and again, and he could feel her shudder beneath him. Deliberately, he slowed, arching more forcefully into her, then pulling out, the way he knew she liked. Bumping her cervix really revved her up, and if he did it right, he could give her several rolling orgasms that way.

"Oh, you bastard," she panted. "I have missed this so bad."

Dev pushed up on his arms to look down at her, grinding his hips hard. Amberly's eyelids fluttered, and even in the dim light from the bathroom he could see the red flushing across her chest. That was a clear sign of her arousal. It had been there yesterday morning when he'd checked her arm, and it had gotten him hard then.

The woman was everything to him.

Sharp fingernails dug into his ass in supplication, and he ground even harder against her, circling, as her pants accelerated. Then, just a few hard strokes in, she arched off the mattress, giving a high, keening cry. The clutch of her body around his felt incredible. Knowing his own orgasm was close, he slowed, doing just enough to keep her body rippling but not enough to bring his own orgasm.

Amberly cried out and fell limp to the bed, her hands gliding up his body and out over his shoulders. Then they circled back and up to his head. Holding his face close, she kissed the fuck out of him, her tongue gliding in and out, doing everything he loved.

Even though he was trying to hold his orgasm back, she was doing everything she could to drag it out of him.

He wasn't going to be able to fight it much longer.

Then she pushed him away.

Grinning, Dev rocked back on his heels, knowing what she wanted. Amberly lifted up, peeling the t-shirt over her head. Before she could even lower her arms, he'd cupped her ribcage in his hands and latched onto one of her breasts, sucking hard. She cupped his head in her hands, pressing her lips to his hair.

After he'd paid attention to both breasts, she drew away, and positioned herself diagonally across the mattress, face down. Then she spread her legs and lifted her ass to him.

Dev almost came right then. He gripped his cock in his hand and forced the orgasm to recede. Once he thought he had himself under control, he leaned over her. The position was perfect because when he guided his dick forward, he was perfectly in line with her hot, wet pussy. This was a very dangerous position, though. His dick glided over the inside of her pubic bone here, which was good for both of them. But it was too good. Within just a few gliding strokes, he was right back on the edge of orgasm. And she was grinding her ass up into him, trying to get him to hit deeper.

"I want you to fuck me, Devlin Kreed," she moaned. "Now!"

All thoughts of prolonging the interlude left, and Dev let

his body go. He slammed into her, over and over, desperation pushing him. He needed this orgasm, more than any other orgasm.

And as it washed over him, it was as perfect as it could be. Amberly cried out beneath him, her body going taut as she came again, her body clutching around his cock. Dev groaned because he didn't think his orgasm was ever going to end, but eventually his body played itself out. He really tried not to slump on top of her, but he did for a second, making her giggle beneath him. Even that movement was too much for his sensitive dick, and his hips jerked into her again.

Once he'd caught his breath, he rolled to the side, smacking her pert ass as he went. Amberly giggled and turned over to nestle against his chest. They were both tacky with sweat, but he didn't care. If she wanted to curl into his arms, he would damn well hold her. His arms had been empty too long.

Dev knew they were on a timeline, but he wasn't going to allow Regent to steal this pleasure from him.

"I've missed laying like this, and being with you," she murmured.

"Me too," he rumbled, breathing in the scent of her hair. Absently, he stroked a hand down her back, then back up. Her skin was so incredibly soft, like a foal's downy coat when it was first born. Her fingers were playing in his chest hair, twirling like she always used to do. Then her arm reached around his waist and squeezed.

They were going to have to talk about where their relationship was going, but it wouldn't be today. "Maybe when this is all over we can get dinner or something."

Amberly looked up at him, resting her chin on his chest. "I would love that. We have to save D.C. and kill a man first."

Devlin grinned. "We'd better get to it, then."

HALF AN HOUR LATER, Amberly was still smiling.

Other people had talked about their exes like they were the worst people on earth, and less than twelve hours ago, she probably would have agreed.

Wasn't it funny how fortune could turn on a dime?

They got cleaned up and repacked, then headed out to the car. Devlin had explained his reasoning about keeping the Charger, and she agreed. Hopefully, they would just blend into the crowd of other Chargers on the road. Once they got closer to where they were going, perhaps they would swap out for a truck.

They settled into the car and pulled their seatbelts on. She felt the crinkle of paper in her pocket. "Oh, I forgot about this," she breathed.

It was the grocery list Zed had been tasked with. Smudged and crumpled, it had about a dozen items on it.

"Urea Nitrate has a line through it," Devlin murmured, pointing. "Charley said some components were already being collected. That's the fertilizer that was used in the '93 World Trade Center bombing, wasn't it?"

"It was," she agreed. "But he's going further. He's got components for scatter bombs on here. They scratched lengths of iron pipe through. Ten penny nails, ball bearings, detonation cord, are all crossed off. He's also got SETA 3 on here, which is a lesser known name of one of the components of Semtex."

Devlin glanced at her sharply as he sped up onto the interstate. "Same shit we used in the teams to blow stuff up."

Amberly nodded. "Yup. It's not crossed off, so I assume

that's what they were approaching the Russians for. So, even though he didn't get the Semtex, or maybe *more* Semtex, he still has all the makings for an incredibly destructive pipe bomb. It would have to be hand carried, though. Which means he has to have people willing to be suicide bombers."

"Holy hell... I wish we knew what was inside those cell phones. They could be little tiny charges of Semtex. If he had a way to wire the electronic trigger to only go off when he texted or called..." his voice trailed off.

"...the phones would be completely safe until he lost patience with his people or something," she continued. She looked out the window for a moment. "He's completely egomaniacal. He has all that power in his hand."

"Yes," Devlin agreed. "And there's no way to know how many of these phones he handed out. "

"Nope."

"You need to send a copy of that to Brown and fill him in."

Amberly thought so as well, so she took his phone and snapped a picture, then sent it to her boss, explaining what it was.

"Send that pic to Charley, too, just in case."

Amberly found her in the contacts and felt a little guilty about glancing back through their history. There wasn't much there, mostly him giving updates. Her opening message to him had been *Moon Devil,* obviously to get his attention. Who the hell was this woman?

Switching screens, she typed off a text to Brown to keep her computer use incognito.

Give me five minutes.

Researching on the computer would be a hell of a lot easier than on a borrowed phone.

16

The drive to Bozeman seemed to take an inordinately long time. There wasn't a lot of traffic, but somewhere ahead there had been a crash, because the interstate was at a standstill.

"I hope we get there soon," Amberly murmured, looking up from her laptop screen. She'd been clacking away for the past two hours, researching and collating data.

Dev looked at Amberly and grinned. "Everything is working out the way it needs to, babe."

She cocked her head at him, stretching her neck muscles. "Why do you say that?"

"Haven't you noticed? It's the new moon tonight. It will be completely dark. Perfect stalking time for the Moon Devil."

Amberly rolled her eyes at him. "Whatever. It's going to be black as pitch and unless you have NVGs, you're gonna be bumbling around in the dark like the rest of us."

Hm. She was right. He didn't even have anything like that, even at home. After he'd been charged, he'd given everything over to the evidence techs. It didn't matter. He hadn't wanted any ties to them at all after that.

There were civilian grade optics available, and he'd have to put it on his card, but it might be better than nothing. Being Montana, they might be able to find a decent hunting store that carried that kind of stuff. One of his fellow teammates had been from Billings. It would have been nice to have the option to call him for support.

"The stores will be opening soon in Billings. We have time to gather up some stuff before we head on to Bozeman."

What should have been a two-hour trip to Billings ended up taking a little more than three, and they had two more hours to get to Bozeman. But they took the time to stop at a hunting store just off the interstate. They had small night vision spotting scopes, but they were nothing compared to what he was used to.

"Beggars can't be choosers, I guess," he murmured to Amberly as he carried the bag from the store. He knew the scope would fit on his rifle, but he hated going into the field with unfamiliar equipment.

Once they got to Bozeman, they found a motel on the north side of the city and checked in. They had to use his card for that as well, because they were damn near out of cash. Now that he'd committed to using the card, he could get cash out. It would just tell everyone where he was.

"Fuck it," he said, pocketing his wallet. "We're going to get him tonight, anyway."

Amberly nodded. "We almost have to. Since we don't know how the attack, or attacks, are going down, we have to assume that they'll be leaving Bozeman soon. We have to find him, or at least his camp."

"How far are we from that location on Zed's phone?"

Amberly pulled up the map on his phone. "Looks like less than half an hour, but straight up into the mountains. We're going to need a four by four."

Amberly spread everything they had out on the table, the pictures, the list, her laptop and the file on Regent and his followers. "The answers have to be here."

They pored over everything they had. Dev kept coming back to the picture they'd been calling the spider. "Can you pull up the Virginia Railway Express maps for D.C.?"

They didn't look similar.

"Oh, maybe the Washington Metro..." she murmured, typing in the search terms. The bus map popped up. "That's completely wrong." Then she clicked on the train maps. "Oh, we found it! That's a match!"

Yes, it was. "Okay, so he's sending people in on trains. I bet if we look at the destination points, they'll coincide with a lot of these targets."

She scanned again, nodding slowly. "Yes, I think you're right."

He rested a hand on her shoulder as he stood behind her. "We're figuring it out."

"I need to let Brown know."

Even as she said it, he was typing a message off to Charley. He didn't know if she had any pull in that area, but if they could get someone on those trains, watching, maybe someone would spot something.

He also told her he was moving in tonight if he could find a decent ride and a few more supplies.

Roger that.

Amberly had activated the second burner phone and called Brown. Dev listened as she related the details they'd worked out. Then she paused, and her face fell. "No way," she breathed, her eyes flicking up to his.

Dev could see the shock in her expression, and he wished she'd put the phone on speaker.

"Okay. That's good, at least. Yes, sir. No, we're going in tonight."

She paused, her eyes dropping to her laptop, though she wasn't really seeing. "I knew you would. That's why I didn't say anything. Yes, sir."

And she hung up the phone. "He's not happy you're involved, but he says as long as I stay in charge, we'll be okay."

Dev looked at her incredulously. "Seriously? He wants you to pull rank on me?"

She shook her head, sighing. "I have no idea. And they think they figured out who the granddaughter belongs to."

"Who," he demanded.

"Alfred J. Hatchett."

Dev could have been blown over by a feather. "No way! Old Man Hatchett? Your old boss? Seriously? Has anybody even seen him since he retired?"

"I don't know. Brown didn't say how he learned the information."

That was a little shocking. The Old Man had been tough and thorough, but Dev never would have thought he would work against the country in any way. He'd been patriotic to the bone, first being a Marine, then working for the Agency for more than thirty years. "That sounds so out of character..." Dev murmured.

Amberly looked at him, her eyes troubled. "I know. It's not sitting well with me, either."

"I wonder who researched it?"

She shook her head. "He didn't say."

They continued digging, Dev eventually getting on and

plugging in the address they'd found on Zed's GPS. It looked like it was a cattle ranch. For some reason, he'd thought it was going to be an encampment in the woods. Actually, it was a ranch at the base of a mountain. There were a few pics online he found connected to a young girl's Instagram account.

He created an account and logged into the property valuation office, but he couldn't find the address even listed. Hm.

Dev supposed he'd be going in blind. He only needed to get close enough to take a shot.

To that end, he unboxed his rifle, put it together, and mounted the scope. He wouldn't know until tonight how well it worked. He didn't have Kevlar anymore, or anything even comparable, so he would be going in very exposed. Dev had a feeling there would be more than one target, and he also knew they would be loaded for bear.

His chances of making it out alive were not great. And if they had a gun in their hands, they were enemies.

Anxiety churned in his gut at the thought of what was coming tonight. When you were a part of a team, you had guys to depend upon. When Dev had been on missions, he'd normally had a spotter with him, someone to call out ranges on his shots as well as watch his back. He'd have armor to drive in to the target and armor to drive him out. And the entire team to support.

Dev didn't even want to take Amberly in with him. Not that she wouldn't be great support. She would be. But he had a feeling that when it got down to the nitty-gritty, she would want to try to apprehend Regent rather than kill him.

Dev wanted to leave her behind just to keep her safe, but he knew that wasn't going to happen either.

He was getting his pistol ready when his phone buzzed on the table. Picking it up, he swiped his thumb across.

You have a delivery.

Hm. Stepping to the door, he peered through the security hole, but didn't see anyone standing there. Cautiously, he opened the door and peeked out.

There was a kitted out flat black 4x4 Jeep four-door truck parked in the spot directly in front of the door. It was a damn fine piece of equipment, and seemed to be tempting him. Maybe he could 'borrow' it for tonight.

Then he caught sight of the key fob ring around the antennae. Seriously? Was this for him to use?

He looked around, trying to see who it might belong to. There were a few people moving around at the end of the building, but they were unloading a Tahoe. He pulled the key fob off the antennae and hit the button. It beeped and the lights flashed.

"What's going on?" Amberly asked, stepping beside him.

"I think Charley is my long, lost fairy godmother," he murmured.

Moving to the driver's side door, he pulled it open. There was a Post-it note on the steering wheel. *Don't forget to check the back!*

Devlin looked at the Jeep. It was fairly new and had so many bells and whistles... He could take this thing into the woods for weeks at a time and not need much more than what was on his back. Amberly opened up the passenger side. "Do you see this? It's exactly what we need for tonight."

She nodded, glancing around the interior. "She knew we were going to need something."

Stepping out of the car, he moved to the back and looked in the bed.

"No fucking way..." he breathed, reaching out his hand. It was his kit from the SEALs. And his khaki rifle case. Lifting it from the back, he turned it in his hands. "I need to get inside and look at this."

Activating the lock button on the key fob, he checked their surroundings. It was literally like this stuff had dropped out of the heavens for them. As soon as he was inside the motel room, with the door locked behind them, he sank down into the chair.

"How the fuck did she get this," he asked Amberly as she sat on the corner of the bed.

"Maybe it was in evidence lockup?"

Unzipping the long case, Dev paused. If it wasn't his rifle, he was going to be damned disappointed. Lifting the lid, he exhaled a quivering breath, excitement and relief running through him. *Now* they had a fighting chance. He ran his hand over the desert stock, feeling the divots in the plastic from the many beatings it had taken, banging against rocks and other equipment. But as damaged as the exterior was, the interior mechanics of the weapon ran like a German clock. He'd made sure of that. Or at least they had when he'd been the keeper. Pulling the pieces from the case, he studied them thoroughly. His life would depend upon this gun in a few hours.

"It looks perfect," he murmured. "I don't think anyone has shot this weapon since I had it in my hands."

"It was used in the commission of a hit. It was kept in lockup somewhere," Amberly said softly.

Yes, he could understand that.

"Requiem, right?"

Dev looked down at the gun. "Yes, Requiem. I thought it was appropriate to name it for a ceremony for the dead."

Putting the pieces of the rifle together by muscle

memory, he relished in the feel of it in his hands. Taking a life was never done lightly, and he'd never disrespected the dead. Some of the men in the teams had called the gun 'Wreck'em' for the destruction it wrought, but in his mind it was always Requiem, and he treated it with the respect it deserved.

Slowly, carefully, he put the rifle back into the case, and dragged his pack over. Everything from his boots to his vest to his green boonie hat was there. All his stuff. The NVG goggles were in their nylon case. It barely even looked like anyone had gone through it. "This is so weird," he murmured. "It's like I just went back in time three years."

Amberly nodded. "I bet. Must be nice to have a Charley as a fairly godmother…"

He grinned. "It's not bad…"

There was a black backpack clipped onto the side of his kit, and he unfastened it. Inside, he found a smaller Kevlar vest and a second pair of NVGs. "I think this is for you, babe."

Amberly looked down at the equipment incredulously, then with excitement. "Seriously?"

She fit the vest over her head and fastened the Velcro. It fit her perfectly.

Perception was a funny thing. An hour ago, he'd been looking at a daunting job with very little chance of success. Now he felt like they actually had a chance.

"Let's go kick some ass," he grinned.

Amberly gave him a fist bump. "Hell, yeah."

17

G PS led them along a dirt road skirting the base of a mountain. The ranch that was semi-outlined on Google would start in about three miles, but it was bordered by another dirt road that ran straight up into the mountain. That was where Devlin wanted to be. If he could get to the high ground and scope out the terrain a little bit, he would have the advantage.

It was late afternoon. The sun had already dipped beyond the mountain, giving Dev enough light to see but not outline himself in any way. The Jeep bounced along the track, ready for anything. Unable to help himself, Dev glanced to the side, trying to watch Amberly's boobs bounce, but the vest wouldn't allow that.

"Quit it, you letch," she laughed. "Let's get through tonight, then we'll talk about us."

"Agreed."

She was right. They needed to concentrate on what was before them.

Dev watched for any kind of lookouts or security cameras. He probably wouldn't see them at this speed, but if

they had game cams or the like, they wouldn't see the
images until after the fact. As far as he could see, there were
no power lines up here at all. They looped around a hairpin
curve, and he knew he was where he wanted to be. Driving
off the road and into the woods, he navigated toward the
east, between trees and rocks and scrub. As they neared a
rock embankment he'd noticed on the satellite map, he
turned the Jeep around and shut off the ignition.

Climbing from the Jeep, he headed toward the rock
embankment to look down on the ranch nestled in the
valley below them. Sitting on his ass, he braced his elbows
on his bent knees and peered through his binoculars. This
place looked to be a working cattle ranch. Rusty coated
cattle numbering in the hundreds dotted the fields between
them. Horses were in corrals near the huge, two story
wooden barn. After searching for records through official
channels for more than an hour last night, they'd determined that the place must belong to one of Regent's father's
friends, Landon Smith. The man was older, in his seventies,
but his son Chris was Regent's age, almost forty. Amberly
had found several pictures of Chris, but there was no
mention of him in the original case file or the pictures that
Necco had gotten out. Chris Smith had to be a new follower,
willing to put everything on the line for Regent's wild
conspiracies and terroristic tendencies.

They watched the comings and goings of the ranch for
more than an hour, and when the night faded, he drew out
the NVGs that had been in his pack. He'd had to replace the
battery pack, but that was a small thing to have this
convenience.

"Are you looking at that building off on the far side,
almost across from us?" Amberly murmured.

"Yes."

He wasn't surprised she'd noticed the cabin in the woods on the far side of the valley. Several trucks were parked outside, and armed men had been coming and going. A few women, as well. And then a figure stepped out onto the porch that he recognized, both from dreams and nightmares and from real life.

Cole Regent.

Dev was too far away to see the features of his face, and more importantly, to take the shot, but he recognized the man's body shape and the way he moved as he walked down from the porch to look into the back of a truck. There was a lot of nodding and laughing as about six men leaned on the rails of the truck, looking inside.

"We need to figure out what's in that truck," he murmured. "White Ford, Montana plate, Echo Charley Tango one three two."

"Got it," Amberly murmured. "I'll send it to Brown. Maybe he can get a local on it for a traffic stop."

He read her off three other plate numbers he could see at least partially, then started giving descriptions of the men he could discern.

"A couple of those match descriptions of known associates of Regent, a couple are new."

A car was driving from what looked to be the main house and down the main drive of the ranch, toward town. It was a maroon SUV with two people inside, but with the glare of the headlights, the NVGs couldn't see the plate. Dev swung his focus back up to the cabin.

One of the men were moving to the door of the truck. Inside, Dev could see a packed duffle. "I think they might be moving out tomorrow. He has a stuffed bag in the front seat."

"Damn it," she murmured. "So, it's tonight or nothing."

"Seems like it. I'm heading down."

Dev pushed to his feet, then held a hand down to Amberly, pulling her up beside him. She'd clipped her dark hair back to keep it out of her eyes, and she wore the darkest clothes she had, with the vest over top. If he worked things right, she wouldn't be anywhere near the action, but there was no sense drawing attention to herself. They had earpieces in, again, thanks to Charley, and he'd showed her how to use them.

"I'll update you as much as I can. My plan is to head to the main barn and try to get a viewpoint there. That's close enough to the cabin I can take a shot if I get it."

She nodded, her luminous silver eyes dilated from the dark of the night. Reaching out, she rested her hands on his vest. "I need you to be more careful than you ever have before," she murmured. "I don't like separating, but I understand the need. Just know that if you call, I'm hauling ass in there and blasting you out."

He gave her a grin. "I know you will, babe. I expect you to."

Then he kissed her, slow and deep. It was a promise to her that he would do his best, because they had so much to get back to. If they both made it out alive, he would be back in her life again.

Amberly drew in a ragged breath as she pulled back, but Dev wrapped her in a hug. "Don't worry, babe. We'll get this done."

She nodded against his chest, but he could feel the doubt in her. "Give me an hour to get to the barn. Watch what's going on down there. If anything happens, let me know. In half an hour, go ahead and start down the mountain. Then park in that spot I showed you. That'll put you about five minutes from the front gate."

She nodded, her eyes filling with tears.

"Hey, now, none of that. We're going to get this fucker, and we're going to save a lot of people. If I miss and he takes off, you're the secondary, you understand? You chase him down and do what you have to do."

"I will," she breathed. "But you're not going to miss."

Dev gave her a crooked smile, appreciating the faith she had in him. Then he turned and moved back to the truck. Grabbing his pack, he swung it over his shoulders and fastened it tight over the Kevlar. He'd loaded as many mags as he had. His Beretta was in his thigh holster, and he would carry Requiem over his right shoulder. Strapping his helmet on, he mounted his NVGs so that he could navigate.

The legality of what he was doing bothered him for about three seconds. Yes, he was planning to kill a man without the protection of being in the SEALs. Probably more than one. But it was literally for the greater good. The one thing that Brown had come back with was that most of the targets on Regent's list were confirmed to be places frequented by the wives and children of more than three dozen political leaders. Senators, Congressman, the Speaker of the house. The Vice President's daughter attended Riverview Preparatory.

If he and Amberly failed and didn't check in before morning, there was a plan in place. They would begin evacuating, but if they did, their hands would be tipped and it would all fall apart. Regent and his followers would disperse to the winds and they would have to start over.

It was now or never.

"I love you, Amberly," he said quietly.

With an almost-sob, she threw her arms around him. "I know you do. I love you too. Come back to me."

"I will, my heart."

And he took off at a slow jog, dodging rocks and tree limbs with the help of the NVGs. No one would see him coming down the mountain, unless they had thermal optics. And unless they were actively hunting, thermals weren't something most people carried.

Dev's heart was thudding strongly, and he was glad he'd kept up with his physical conditioning as much as he had. As long as he didn't break an ankle on a rock, he'd be good to go.

Dev made it to the base of the mountain and the ground began to level off. Skirting around a large herd of cattle, he made sure not to disturb them with his passing. He startled one mama with her calf nestled beneath a tree. They took off running.

"Most of the men seem to have settled on the porch of the cabin. I can't tell if Regent is still there or not," Amberly murmured after half an hour. "I'm going to start down the mountain."

"Roger that," he responded. He glanced back once from where he'd come and he thought he saw lights, then they disappeared. The Jeep had been parked so that the headlights wouldn't draw attention when the vehicle was started.

After about an hour of steady jogging, he reached the inner perimeter of fence, around the corrals near the barn. Horses were more aware of their surroundings than cattle, and a few of them snorted at him as he moved close. Dev spoke softly to them, hoping they would think he was just another hand, out for a nightly stroll. They eventually settled down as he passed by.

Before he went over the final plank fence, he crouched behind a black rubber water trough and watched for movement. There were a few lights on in the barn, but it seemed like everything had been buttoned up for the night. It was going on eleven at night, so most people would be looking for their beds, he hoped.

Pulling the NVGs down, he looked away from the barn, into the night. It was quiet. Nothing moved, other than the animals, dozing lazily. Flipping the goggles back up, he jumped the fence and headed for the barn. As soon as he was inside, he flattened himself against the giant sliding door. Then he looked for a way to go up.

"Who are you?" a female voice demanded. "You're in the wrong place."

Dev had spun, Requiem half-raised, as soon as he heard the voice, and his heart sank. It was a young girl, maybe sixteen or seventeen, leaning on the top of a stall door. A gray mare stood behind her, ears pricked forward.

"You people know he's up in the cabin. We've told you to stay away from the animals," she continued. Then she narrowed her eyes as she looked him over. "You're not with the Blade. Who are you? Are you going to take the asshole out?"

"Yes," he said simply.

The girl grinned and gave a funny little dance. "Finally. If he tells me one more time I would be a good wife for one of his men, I was going to shoot him myself. You can do it for me."

Dev snorted. "I'll try. I'm trying to be quiet here, though."

"Oh, yeah," the girl's voice dropped as she let herself out of the stall. "I get you. Can I help? He's screwed my dad up."

Dev looked at her. Typical ranch kid, dirty boots and jeans. "Your dad is Chris?"

She nodded. "Cole showed up about a month ago and started making himself at home, telling dad these crazy stories. Even I know they're fake news." She rolled her eyes for emphasis. "Dad's had to take over the ranch, though, and he's having problems with the DNR not renewing his lease and stuff."

"I'm sorry."

Dev felt ridiculous standing here in his full kit, weapon in hand, just tempting fate to send another fucking witness. "Listen, you need to go to the house and tuck in. Pretend you never saw me. You hear me?"

Threatening a kid was out of the question, but he could strenuously suggest.

"I hear you." She glanced down at his gun, and something went over her face. "Wow, you really are here to shoot him. I think he's doing bad things, so you should."

She stared up into Dev's face for a long moment, before motioning to the far corner. "If you need to go high, those are the stairs. On that far wall," she pointed beyond his shoulder, "there's a ladder up to the cupola. It's not very big, but it's sturdy, and you can see everywhere on the ranch."

Dev swallowed and gave her a single nod. "Go in the house and lock up. Who was it that left a while ago?"

"That was the housekeeper and her son. They always leave later."

"Okay," Dev murmured. "You should go. Lock the doors and don't let anyone in. If you hear gunfire, take cover."

"Don't shoot my dad," the girl pleaded. "I think he's up there with him."

Wincing, Dev shifted. "You need to try to get him down to the house. If he shoots at me..."

The girl blinked her big eyes. "I understand. I'll try."

Unable to do otherwise, he gave her a nod. "And I'll try not to kill him if he stays," he promised. "Go get safe."

The girl took off at a run, dust flying up behind her boot

heels. Devlin watched until she got into the house before heading for the stairs. "Did you catch all that?"

Amberly laughed on the other end of the line. "Yes. Way to put you in a pickle."

"I'm not in a pickle," he murmured. "If he raises a weapon in support of Regent, I'm going to drop him."

"Yes."

"Are you down the mountain?"

"I am," she confirmed. "Ready to tear in and get you."

"Okay. Love you, babe."

"Love you too," she breathed.

Then he turned the com unit off. He needed to concentrate for a while.

Climbing the stairs into the hayloft, he tried to be quiet. Hopefully, the girl would stay in the house and keep her mouth shut about seeing him. Just in case she didn't, though, he needed to hurry up and get into position. The secondary ladder was where she said it was, and he climbed up to a plank walkway, which spanned the width of the barn. Right in the center was another ladder up into the cupola. It was a tight fit, but he managed to get situated, pushing one of the little vented doors open. Then he fit the muzzle of Requiem through the opening.

This was perfect.

There was a bit of an angle up to the cabin, but the wind was quiet. He put his eyes to the night vision scope and focused.

Half a dozen men sat on the front porch of the cabin. Dev wondered if it had been a manager's cabin, or something. Maybe an old bunkhouse, and they were all staying there. One of the men stood and walked out into the yard, answering a call. Was that Chris? For the girl's sake, Dev hoped the man listened and went home.

Within just a few minutes, after talking to the men again and laughing, the man headed down to the main house and disappeared inside.

The timing wasn't going to get much better. Yes, there were a lot of men on the porch, but if they all decided to turn in and headed inside, it would be a lost shot.

Snugging the weapon to his shoulder, he plotted out the targets. Regent would be first, of course, then he'd work to the right, where the easier targets were. Even though he had a suppressor on the end of the weapon, as soon as he fired, he would be exposed. There was only so much muzzle flash and noise that could be obscured. He expected return fire.

Dev took a few deep breaths, his heart racing. Finally, after all this time, he was going to take out Cole Regent, the man who had basically destroyed his life, whether or not he realized it. Dropping the crosshairs onto his head, Dev rested his finger on the trigger, and slowly squeezed.

18

Amberly had the windows rolled down and the truck off hoping to hear anything from the ranch. Devlin had turned off the coms unit, but she breathed shallowly in case she missed a whisper or other sound.

Her gut was churning, and she didn't know how to make it better. So much was riding on this night. They needed a twelve-man CIA Insertion team to effectively carry out this plan. Instead, it was just the two of them, and Dev was doing the bulk of the work at this second.

Did she drive up the driveway in the hopes of being closer in case he needed her? No, because if she did that, somehow they would miss each other. She would wait until he called her, then get in there as fast as she could.

Getting out of the car, she paced along beside it for about ten feet, then crossed back. She was so worried for Devlin. So much had changed in four days.

This was a stupid plan. They should have waited until Regent was leaving and take him out on the truck or something. Instead, Devlin was in the middle of the hornet's nest.

Grabbing her phone, she looked for a text or anything. Nothing. Brown had her new burner number. That niggling thought bugged her again. How had he learned about Hatchett's granddaughter?

She typed off a message to Brown, asking him.

Frank heard I was looking and said he helped find them a place out there. We've got a team on the ground in Antigua looking for him.

Amberly's stomach twisted. Frank. Her friend. Or at least, she thought he was her friend. Frank Callypso had been there for her her entire professional career. When everything had gone down with Devlin, he'd been a literal shoulder to cry on. She'd eaten meals at his house with his wife, and listened to him complain about his kids moving away.

Frank had been in charge of the escort team the night Regent was moved. If he'd known SAC was going to remove Regent... then he'd probably known that Devlin was going to be set up as the fall guy.

Her heart ached at the thought of her friend taking part in terroristic activities. Yeah, he'd bitched about some of the country's policies. More often, he bitched about the politicians. Had it been such an anger that it would impel him to take action against the country she thought he loved?

She stared down at the message on her phone.

Brown, where is Frank now?

He's taking a couple of days off. It's he and his wife's anniversary.

No, it wasn't, but Brown, who'd only been there a short time, wouldn't realize that. *His anniversary is in May, right after his wife's birthday.*

The phone rang in her hand. "So, what are you saying, Temple?"

"There are enough inconsistencies that I believe Frank Callypso might be Regent's inside CIA man."

"Fuck, that's what I thought you were saying. Let me do some digging."

"See if you can ping his phone."

"Just a minute," Brown murmured, and it sounded like he was holding the cell phone with his chin. She heard computer keys clacking. Then a long silence. "Temple. His phone was last at a Bozeman, Montana tower."

"Are you fucking kidding me," she hissed. "What the fuck do I do?"

Brown sighed on the other end of the line. "I'm going to continue digging, but right now, the fact that he's out there and not because of you makes me think he's in collusion with known domestic terrorists."

Her eyes burned, and she blinked. Frank Callypso, her mentor and friend, was playing dirty.

DEV SQUEEZED THE TRIGGER... just as some guy ran up the steps of the porch, fouling his shot. That man went down, and he saw Regent jerk, then lunge to the side for cover. So, he'd hit him, but hadn't killed him.

"Fuck," he hissed, acquiring the next target. The man sitting beside Regent with a beer in his hand never even moved as he died, just dropped the beer. One man sailed off the edge of the porch and Dev caught him in the neck. He skidded on his face and was still. Dev jerked his scope back to where Regent had gone down, but his view was obscured by a truck. He scanned back and forth, very carefully controlling his breathing.

Where the fuck had he gone?

There was movement at the back of the truck as someone started shooting an automatic AR 15. They were firing wild, though. They hadn't actually seen where he was, just thought they knew. There was a small building down the hill from the cabin they were aiming and firing at.

Dev took the shooter out, watched as another man peered out from behind a vehicle and started to fire. At the very least, he'd ruined most of Regent's plan by taking out these men.

By his count, he'd killed four and wounded two. The first guy might still be alive, though he had to be in pain.

Dev debated dropping down from the barn and hustling up there. It was less than half a mile, but he would be exposed.

A truck sped up the drive and for a moment he thought it was Amberly, arriving early. But the vehicle turned up the hill to the cabin, and Dev realized it was trying to rescue Regent.

"Oh, no, you don't," he said, taking aim.

He couldn't see the front wheels, but the back wheels were easy enough to take out. The car skidded wildly, but still seemed sound enough to pick someone up and turn back down the hill. Surely that had been Regent getting into the car... Aiming at the driver's side of the windshield, he plowed round after round into it. The car suddenly accelerated as it slammed into the plank fence and jounced into the field, coming to rest against a tree.

That had been a devastating crash, and Dev doubted anyone would make it out. Pivoting, he scanned the area around the deck. There was a man on the ground waving his hand weakly, but that was the only movement.

He keyed on his coms unit. "Come get me. We have some cleanup to do."

"Roger that," Amberly said, voice calm.

Dev watched for another minute, waiting to hear the Jeep roaring up the driveway before he started making his way down through the hayloft. A couple of the horses nickered as he jogged through the barn and out the big door he'd originally come through. Amberly was there, parked at a hitching post.

It wasn't easy getting into the passenger side of the Jeep, but he managed it, stowing Requiem on the back seat. Pulling his sidearm, he pointed for her to drive.

"We need to check that vehicle."

She gassed the Jeep and they tore through the grass and gravel. She followed the path the previous truck had and looped wide around the tree. Slamming it into park, they both tumbled out, weapons up, and crept up the sides of the crumpled mass. Amberly took the driver's side, Dev the passenger.

"This one isn't going anywhere," she said, peering in at the corpse.

"Neither is this one. And it's not Regent. It's one of the brothers."

"And this is the other one," she confirmed.

Just then they heard the roar of an engine, but it sounded different. They turned toward the cabin just in time to see a side by side ATV take off behind the cabin.

"You shoot, I drive," Amberly called, darting for the open door of the Jeep.

Dev wasn't even settled by the time she took off back

through the crashed fence. "Stop at the cabin. I have to see if it's Regent."

The Jeep roared as it climbed the drive, then skidded as Amberly hit the brakes next to the truck the Blade had been using for cover. Dev jumped out and circled the bed, weapon up and ready. There were bodies everywhere, but none of them were Regent. He looked at the chair where the man had been sitting. Yes, there was a significant amount of blood on the wood, but not enough to debilitate him, obviously.

Dev scrambled up the steps and into the cabin, pushing the door wide.

And took a shotgun blast to the chest.

Dev flew back across the front porch and landed on his back at the base of the steps. A man staggered out of the cabin, gun raised, blood coating his front. He staggered, gaze locked on Dev, and took a bullet through the neck from Amberly's gun, then another through the chest. He collapsed where he stood.

Then Amberly was there, peering down at him. "Get your ass up, you're fine. Your vest took the shot."

Dev gasped in air, gritting his teeth. Amberly ran up the porch steps and through the door, leaping over the body. She returned seconds later, as he was surging to his feet. The Beretta was still in his hand, miraculously.

"No one else in there. All the info on the bombings is, though. That must have been Regent taking off."

She jerked on his vest, pulling him up, getting his legs moving. "Let's go, Moon Devil. You've got work still to do."

They clambered into the Jeep and Amberly followed the path of the ATV. It was easy enough to see, even in the dark, because it was lined with pine trees. Gunning the truck, they surged up the mountain. The Jeep wasn't as nimble as the ATV probably, but it definitely had more power, and on this narrow track, power was more important for the moment.

Then they broke through the trees and into a meadow, it looked like. Amberly had to slow to get a direction of travel. The ATV, and its bouncing tail lights, had gone to the right, still climbing. She followed the path of crushed grass several hundred yards until it disappeared into another stand of pine. This track was even narrower, tree limbs scraping the sides of the truck. Dev held onto the 'oh shit' handle as Amberly expertly drove through an increasingly cluttered path. At one point, they jounced over a pine tree on the ground, bucking them up out of their seats.

When they broke out of the pines, Amberly had to slam on the brakes. They skidded right to the edge of a rocky embankment. "Fuck," Amberly breathed.

His own balls might have sucked up a little as well, because that was a hell of a drop-off. "Good job, babe!"

Grinning, Amberly backed away from the cliff and turned. There was a narrow track running along the edge of the rock wall. "Will we fit?"

"Hope so," she murmured, guiding the Jeep to follow.

It looked like it used to be a damn horse path. Then ATV or dirt bikes started using it, widening the path a little. He didn't know if it was wide enough for a full-sized Jeep though.

Amberly was focused on the track, mouth open, breathing heavily as she concentrated completely on keeping them alive. She flinched as the driver's side mirror hit a rock outcrop and flipped into the door. Dev was impressed that she kept it so close to the rock wall, because his side was a near vertical drop.

Then, suddenly, the road opened up and they seemed to be on a plateau or something. It was damn near level.

That was when the gunshots sounded. They both ducked, but Amberly continued to drive forward, bouncing over rocks and through depressions. They were a big, bright target coming across the field in the pitch black night.

That gave him an idea. "Turn off your lights," he commanded her.

"What," she screeched.

"Just do it!"

Amberly turned the lights off on the Jeep and turned to the right, getting out of the line of fire. Then he flipped the NVGs down over her eyes. "Sorry about that, babe."

"Oh, dude. Hell yeah!"

Spinning the wheel, she floored the truck, taking sharp turns and hitting her brakes as they drove through the night. Bullets stopped hitting them, and Dev knew they had to be damned close to Regent.

Suddenly, lights flared as the ATV came to life. Amberly gasped as the light overwhelmed the AVGs and pushed them off her head. She blinked several times in the darkness, then the chase was on again.

Dev tried to take aim out the window, but his hand bounced like crazy. There was no way he'd get a decent shot off.

Then he heard something over the sound of the vehicle engines. It sounded like rotors from a chopper.

"Is that a helicopter," Amberly cried, glancing around.

"I think so. Keep after him. This must have been his escape plan all along."

Amberly stomped on the gas and the truck leaped forward. Dev wasn't sure how the fuck she kept it going in a fairly straight line, the way it was bouncing around. The only comfort he took was in that the ATV was probably having just as hard of a time as they were as they climbed the mountain.

The sound of the helicopter built as it flew over top of them, closer than was comfortable. A spotlight flipped on, blinding in its intensity, but Amberly never wavered. The chopper flew on, spotlit the ATV for them, then swooped up the mountain. Whoever the pilot was, he was doing a damned good job.

"Frank is dirty," she called, glancing at him.

"Callypso?" he asked incredulously.

She nodded. "That's his granddaughter in Fort Collins. He's had his nose in everything, and I was too blind to see it."

"Is he working with Regent voluntarily or by force?"

"I think voluntarily, but that Regent was looking for leverage on him."

Yeah, that made sense. He looked at Amberly. "Are you okay?"

Anger flashed in her eyes. "Yeah, I'm fine. Kind of half hoping that he's in the chopper. Brown says his phone pinged in Bozeman, so he's around."

"Fuck," he breathed.

Amberly hit a depression in the field and they ramped out of it, then it seemed to smooth out. She laid on the gas, plunging up a rocky hillside. The ATV was only a few dozen yards ahead, tires spitting gravel as it climbed.

Amberly shifted the Jeep into a lower gear as gravity began to pull. This was a steep hill. As slow as they were going, though, it gave him a chance to take aim and fire at the ATV. Several of his hits struck, but in the dark, it was hard to guesstimate where the tires were. And if he hit the tires, it may not make much difference on this hill.

The climb began to level out as they crested a rise. The helicopter was hovering, spotlight scanning the dark night. The ground sloped down to a small cleared spot, just big enough for the chopper to land.

"Stop, Amberly."

She hit the brakes and skidded to a stop. Dev scrambled out and reached in the back for Requiem. "Don't foul my shot," he warned her, and she grinned at him, taking off after the ATV. Absolute terror filled him, because she was going so fast down the hill. If she didn't slow down, she could go over the edge. Was she going to ram him?

A man scrambled from the ATV and starting staggering for the helicopter.

Dev dropped to the ground. They had to end this, now. Amberly was giving everything she had to stop a madman, and he could do no less.

Centering himself, he took aim on the chopper. There was a light on in the cockpit and he could see the pilot. Breathing out, Dev tried to focus on the chopper's trajectory, settling to the ground. There was a second man leaning out the door with a weapon, but he was more invested in the pilot. No pilot, no fly away.

He squeezed his finger on the trigger.

Two things happened at once.

Dev heard Amberly strike something with the Jeep, then the skittering of gravel as she hit her brakes. The Jeep, as hardy as it was, couldn't stop at that speed and he watched in horror as the vehicle slid off the side of the mountain.

19

A mberly knew she was fucked.

     The Jeep had done them well, but she'd been going too fast as she'd struck Cole Regent when he got out of the ATV. It was worth dying, as long as he was dead. He'd been thrown into the air with the hit, and had landed in a crumpled heap.

Amberly gripped the wheel, fighting to maintain control as the Jeep slid down a rocky incline. Then she hit something hard. Her neck rocked forward and she bumped the steering wheel with her forehead, but the airbags didn't go off. When she looked up, she saw by the light of the headlights that the Jeep had come to rest against a tree.

Allowing herself to take a breath, she did a quick inventory of herself. Her insides felt like a milkshake from the crazy ride up the mountain, then down, and her head hurt, but overall she was okay. Pushing her door open, she looked up the rocky incline, where Devlin might still be fighting.

"Fuck, this is going to hurt," she breathed as she shoved her gun in her holster and started climbing. She was only about twenty feet down the embankment, but it was almost vertical, with loose, jagged rocks to contend with.

She heard the ping of bullet on metal and realized Dev was still firing at the chopper. Pouring on the power, she scrambled up the mountain, determined to be there at the end. They needed to confirm that Regent was dead. And if he was in the chopper, Frank, as well. That made her heart ache, but she turned the emotion off. Frank had chosen his side.

As she neared the top, she slowed and removed her weapon, holding it out in front of her. She lifted her head above the line of the rock, scanning for danger.

The helicopter thumped down just as she got into position. Amazingly, it sat and didn't move, other than the rotors spinning. Dev must have gotten the pilot.

Even as she watched, a big man jumped down out of the chopper, and she recognized him immediately. Frank Callypso. He ran to the crumpled body on the ground, and she knew what he was doing.

Getting her legs under her, Amberly broke into a shambling run across the field. "Frank," she screamed, taking aim.

Frank went still, leaning over Regent's body. Amberly assumed she'd killed the fucker with the Jeep, because he was a bloody mess. Frank had to be looking for the phone, though. Did he honestly think it would do him any good now? None of the people were in place. They were all dead down the mountain. The only people he could possibly kill were the family members of the men already dead.

"They're all dead, Frank."

The older man peered over his shoulder at her. "I know, Amberly. I saw the bodies on the way up here. How did you do that?"

"It doesn't matter. How could you do this?"

Frank sank back on one heel. Amberly couldn't see his hands, but she assumed he'd found the phone. She also assumed Frank had a weapon in his ankle holster, at the very least. He may actually have his main weapon, a Glock, in his hand. She hadn't seen it yet.

"You're the one that got Regent out of prison," she panted. "And Zed. And how many others?"

Frank chuckled. "A few."

"Do you seriously believe in what he was doing?" she asked, moving carefully around so that she could see his face better.

Frowning, he looked down at the man lying dead in front of him. "In a way, yes. Sometimes, when you're so close to it, you don't realize how deep the bullshit gets until you're almost drowning in it. I've been drowning for a long time, so I've done my part to keep the bullshit in line."

"And how is killing family members of domestic terrorists going to help you do that?"

Frank snorted. "I'm not worried about them, although they might want to die just for the hell of it when they realize their family is gone. No, I need the phone to blow up the rest of the devices we've already planted."

Amberly blinked. "What?"

Laughing, Frank pushed to his feet, a black touch screen smart phone in his hand. "Oh, didn't you figure that part out?"

She shook her head, trying to catch up. There was no mention of other explosive devices. Oh, fuck. "How many?" she demanded.

Frank gave her a sly grin. "Oh, I don't know. A dozen. Maybe two. You'd be amazed how many places they let an old CIA officer in."

"And what is your granddaughter going to say when she finds out you were targeting women and children?"

For the first time, she saw some emotion on his face. Sadness, or maybe regret. "She's never going to know I was involved."

"Oh, yes, she will. I'll make sure of it," Amberly vowed.

Anger clouded his face, along with determination. "Then I'm going to have to make sure you don't make it off the mountain. Maybe I'll give you a hero's ending, dying while killing the notorious fugitive Cole Regent."

Amberly could tell that Frank was going to make his move, and she prayed Dev was in position. As soon as he lifted his weapon, Dev fired. She didn't hear it, just saw the effect. Frank's body jerked and blood sprayed from the bullet wound in his chest. He looked down incredulously, then crashed to the ground, gasping for air.

Amberly should have felt more, but she didn't. What Frank had chosen to participate in was reprehensible, and she couldn't condone anything that he'd done. At one time, he might have been her friend, but she doubted it. She had a feeling that once they started digging into his actions and movements, they would find all his crimes.

Dev materialized out of the dark and walked into the circle of light from the ATV. Stopping in front of her, he cupped her face in his hands. "Are you okay?"

Amberly nodded, feeling a little numb. A lot had happened in the past hour, and it would take a while to come down off the adrenalin rush. "Are you okay?"

"Yeah. Just wondering how we're going to get out of here."

She mustered a grin for him. "You can't fly a helicopter?"

Dev barked out a laugh. "I might be able to turn it off, but I definitely can't fly."

Lowering his head, he kissed her for a moment, then wrapped her in his arms. Amberly sagged into him, wishing they were in any fucking nameless motel anywhere in the world that had a bed.

"What do we need to do to get the fuck off this mountain?" she murmured.

They turned around to look at the body of Cole Regent and found themselves looking down a wavering gun barrel. Before either one of them could move, the gun fired.

DEV KNEW what was going to happen, and he dove at Regent, taking the shot aimed at Amberly. Burning pain swallowed his leg, giving him extra fury as he landed on top of Regent. The man was mostly dead. There was a gunshot wound high on his chest, surely from Requiem. And several other bruises and abrasions all over, probably from being slapped by tree limbs on the ride up here. The ATV didn't have a windshield or anything.

His legs were obviously broken and he was laying wrong. There was also a bleeding hole in his gut, and Dev wondered if one of the other men managed to shoot him. That would be a story. Turned on in his hour of need by his own people. Even as they watched, he took his last, gasping breath. Kneeling down, Amberly checked for a pulse, then shook her head.

Pulling out his phone, Dev took a picture of the dead man and sent it to Charley.

"Are you okay?" she asked, resting a hand on his shoulder.

Dev nodded, looking down at his leg. A long, thin line

cut through the fabric of his BDUs, but it wasn't bleeding too bad. It was just a scratch.

Frank was gone, the light faded from his eyes. Both of them were angry fools, dead by their own actions.

Reaching for her phone, she took a picture of the dead bodies as well, then a short video, because she knew it would be needed in the investigation later. The burner phone wasn't equipped with a great camera, but it would be better than nothing. Then she sent it to Brown.

Within just a couple of minutes, Brown called. "You got them both?"

"Yes," she confirmed, "along with about seven others. You're going to have to send a clean-up crew out, posthaste."

"I've already got one on the way. I knew something like this would happen."

"Brown," she paused. "There are more bombs. Not just in the phones. I think Frank has been planting them around D.C. We need to look at his movements for the past week to two weeks, at least."

"On it. I expect you to gather all the documentation you can and get it here, pronto."

"I'll do pictures first," she promised. "As soon as I figure out how the hell to get down off this mountain."

They ended up loading Frank and Regent's dead bodies in the back of the ATV. It was the only thing drivable at the moment, though they saw the Jeep wedged against the tree on the way down the mountain.

"I liked that Jeep," Dev grumbled.

His leg was bandaged and Requiem was between his knees, the muzzle pointed up. Amberly was behind the wheel again, but the narrower ATV was a lot easier to drive down the mountain, even in the dark.

There was a lot of work to do once they got to the cabin. Apparently, the shoot-out had drawn enough attention that the law had been called. There was a young Sheriff's deputy taking pictures of the bodies outside with his cell phone, the blue lights of his cruiser flashing in the night. When they parked the ATV near the cabin, they were met with a drawn gun.

"Hands up where I can see them," the kid ordered.

"You're going to want to put your weapon away, deputy," Amberly told him calmly. "This is a CIA operation." Very carefully, she removed her ID from her bag and held it out.

"What the hell happened here, ma'am?" he asked, voice wavering.

"I think it's best if you don't know a lot, Deputy, unless you want to testify in federal court." His eyes widened comically. "This is what I'm going to need you to do."

Within minutes, he was cordoning off the area around the cabin with police tape. Squads had gotten there not long after, as well as the sheriff. Amberly filled him in a little, enough to appease the man and explain why she was using his resources.

"It would have been nice to get a call beforehand so my county could have responded a little better."

Amberly sighed. "Honestly Sheriff, we had no time. If you look in the back of the truck, they're packed and ready to go. They were leaving in hours. And I had to move on the information I'd been given."

The older man sighed. "Yeah, I suppose you're right. It wouldn't have done to have this stuff come out of our state."

Sheriff Belle arranged to have the bomb squad come from Billings to take care of the devices in the back of the truck. He also, very helpfully, arranged for a team to go up and retrieve their Jeep, and catalog evidence on the mountain top. Then, finally, Amberly walked inside the cabin to begin gathering evidence.

20

D ev looked at the amount of data around them, and he shook his head.

The inside of the cabin was lined with diagrams, maps, pictures of people- mostly politicians. He recognized several of the head honchos from Washington, and he didn't watch the news much.

There was a long wooden table where it looked like Cole sat and ran his kingdom of paramilitary fanatics. The man had been like a modern day general, planning out who would go where, the exact time, what train line, what he would carry and who he was to target. He had also written down a master list of demands, meant to be implemented as the devastation began to spread.

Regent wanted to hold the safety of the politician's families over their heads to have emergency measures passed, because he felt like his personal liberties as an American were being eroded away. And he found enough people that believed the same thing to rebel against the government and commit their lives for change. The men were going to be suicide bombers, and Amberly actually found a waiting list of people ready to take their place if something fell through or they backed out.

"My god," he breathed.

The dedication was truly something. She'd never spoken to Cole Regent herself, just saw footage of him from years ago. Obviously, he had refined his pitch, because he went from being a one-man band to compelling hundreds to take part in his madness.

"This guy was something," he said softly.

They were taking pictures of everything and forwarding them on. Hopefully, something in this shit pile would indicate where the charges were that Frank had planted. Because of the September 11th anniversary coming up, it was paramount that they find them.

Dev found the contact name for the Russians, and Amberly forwarded it on to Brown. Maybe he could track down their movements and contacts.

The sun was actually coming up behind them when they finally got ready to leave. The CIA team had arrived and were taking over, wading through piles upon piles of information and names. Amberly and Dev were going to hand carry what appeared to be the most pertinent evidence back to Langley, though it had all been thoroughly photographed.

The Sheriff's team had dropped off the Jeep in front of the barn when they'd come down the mountain. Dev didn't know how they'd gotten it down off that incline without rolling it. Whatever. He was happy to see it, since all their crap was still in it.

Dev didn't know if he even wanted to go back to the D.C. area. After the whole SAC setup three years ago, he was less than thrilled with the thought of being back in Langley and on their home turf. He wanted to be there for Amberly, though.

He needed to ask her what she wanted to do. Actually, they needed to talk about several things.

Tiredness beat at him, though, and he knew they needed sleep. And shower. Eating would be nice.

If he could steal just a few hours of her time before they dove back into the craziness. There were still an unknown amount of explosive devices to be found. And reports to write. People to interview and talk to.

Technically, though, his job was done. It had been his responsibility to rescue Amberly and dispatch Regent, both of which he had completed. In all honesty, he was looking forward to getting back to Tennessee. It had been nice to finish one last mission, but it was time for the younger kids to take over the dangerous stuff.

He glanced over at Amberly. "You okay, babe?"

There was a brittle look to her, like she'd reached the end of her energy and her emotions were near the surface. "Yeah. I'm fine. Just fried."

"Yeah. Too much adrenalin for too long. We're going to go crash for a while."

"Okay," she sighed, resting her head on the back of the seat.

Rather than a cheap motel, Dev pulled into one of the nicer looking tourist hotels in Bozeman. The woman at the registration desk didn't know what to think when she saw them coming in. He was still in his blood-spattered gear, carrying Requiem in the case, along with his duffle. Amberly also had blood all over her, and a purpling knot on her forehead. They were quite the pair.

The woman took his card and assigned them a room, promising breakfast in the morning. They headed around the corner to the elevator. When they stepped off on the fourth floor, their room was just off to the right. Dev keyed the door and they slipped in, dropping bags and gear as they stripped down. Without even talking about it, they both headed to the big, walk-in shower. Dev adjusted the temp and waved her in, grabbing the little bottles of soap and shampoo from the vanity.

The hot water felt amazing, and they took turns basking under the stream. Pouring a dollop of shampoo into his hand, he motioned for Amberly to turn around. Then he lathered her hair, watching as dirt and blood and pine needles swirled down to the drain. It had been a messy business tonight.

They dried each other off with pristine white towels. Dev winced as he saw the remnants of blood from his thigh wound. It wasn't deep, just long and awkward. Amberly painted it with antibiotic, then stretched a bandage along its length, taping it down. It felt weird to move.

"Let me see your head," Dev murmured.

She turned and looked up at him, her eyes squinted with tiredness. The knot was purple, but not too bad. "I think you'll be fine."

Then, finally giving in, they climbed naked beneath the sheets. Dev settled her against his chest and wrapped an arm around her. "I love you, my heart."

"I love you, too," she whispered, and immediately fell asleep.

≈

AMBERLY WOKE to Dev snoring softly in her ear. The sun was doing its best to break through the curtains, and she turned her head away, needing more sleep. Then she realized she had to pee. Sighing, she rolled out of bed, almost crying with pain, and padded to the bathroom. She did her business and paused in front of the mirror. Damn. It looked like she'd been in a brawl. Bruises decorated her from head to toe, and she knew it was from the beating they'd taken racing up the mountain in the Jeep. Then crashing the Jeep. Then crashing the Jeep again.

Walking out to lean against the doorjamb, she looked at Devlin. His face was slack with sleep and grizzled with a beard. His mostly-gray hair was mussed, but he looked relaxed. The blanket was down around his waist, and she had to appreciate the shape he was in, though he was a little bruised as well. The thought of what his body could do to hers woke her up a little, and made her smile.

"What are you thinking, standing there all delicious and bruised?"

Amberly snorted, turning her forearms for him. "I know, right? Look at all these lovely purple things..." Walking forward, she sank to the edge of the bed. "I was thinking that I was very glad you were with me this week. I don't know that I could have done this with anyone else."

Devlin snorted. "I know you couldn't have. It had to be me."

She danced her fingers across his ribs. "Don't be smug."

"I'm not," he laughed, grabbing her hand. He sobered, looking into her eyes. "I'm very glad you were with me as well," he murmured, drawing her down for a kiss.

Amberly let herself sink into it, knowing that they were going to have to deal with bad things in a little while. She needed this moment to just be with him. To remind herself

what she fought for when she dealt with criminals like
Regent. Pushing that out of her mind, she basked in Devlin's
love, and wondered where they went next.

THEY CHECKED out of the hotel at seven that evening, and
were handed a message as they checked out. There was a
private plane at the airport waiting for them that would fly
them directly to Virginia. Once they landed, a car met them
and escorted them to the George Bush Center For Intel-
ligence.

Devlin had gone quiet, and she knew why. This would
be like walking into a den of cobras for him. The last time
he'd been here, he'd been considered a criminal, and she
had no doubt those memories were strong in his mind. "Just
remember," she said as she used her ID to swipe into the
quiet building. "They are in the wrong. They were in the
wrong with you three years ago, and they need to be kissing
your ass. As do I."

Dev gave her a slight smile before turning his badass
SEAL face on.

Amberly didn't even try to go to her own office first. She
headed upstairs to Deputy Director Brown, knowing he
probably had a conference room assigned to the Tango 11
case. And she was right. Despite the late hour, she walked
into a bustling, energetic throng of people wading through
the information she and Devlin had forwarded to them. In
her hands, she carried the box of hard copies. And the
phones.

It startled her when someone started clapping. Then
another person, and another, until the entire room was clapping for her and Devlin. Amberly didn't get embarrassed

very often, but she felt her cheeks heat, and she nodded at people in acknowledgement.

"In my office, Temple," Brown called out. "And you too, Kreed."

Amberly stepped into the office and set the box down on the edge of Brown's desk. The man had never been especially intimidating to her. Short and bald as a cue ball, there was something a little babyish about him. But he'd impressed her this week. Rather than being an irritating asshole, he'd actually been a supportive boss, carrying his load on this end.

"I'm glad to see you two made it back in one piece," he murmured, settling into his leather office chair. He waved for them to sit in the chairs opposite, and she sank down. Devlin stood at the door, unbending. She'd seen that expression in his eyes before, and she knew there would be no coddling or bending him.

"I feel like we should get this out of the way first," Brown murmured, holding a folded letter out to Devlin.

Devlin moved forward and took the paper, unfolding it and scanning. Then he handed it to Amberly. It was a formal apology from the director of the CIA. And a promise to closely monitor the SAC division of the CIA.

"I want to personally apologize as well," Brown murmured. "I know the agency isn't perfect, but this was wrong on many levels."

"You weren't in charge of it," Devlin murmured finally, "so you weren't responsible. No apology needed."

Brown shrugged and didn't look convinced, but he turned his attention back to Amberly. "We're going through Frank's life with a fine-tooth comb right now. His wife is devastated, but kind of not surprised. She said she'd noticed him being 'off' and distracted. More complaining. She thought it was another case that had him on edge. She doesn't seem to be involved with the operation, though."

Amberly frowned. Anna was a good woman, and she didn't deserve what Frank had done to her. She didn't deserve this scrutiny. Once things kind of settled down, maybe she'd go talk to her.

"We haven't found any of the bombs he supposedly planted," Brown said, "and nothing in any of the pictures..."

His voice trailed off as if in question, so Amberly treated it as such. "I don't think Regent knew about them. I think this was Frank's own side-project."

Brown sighed, and she could see tiredness in his expression. It was obvious he'd burned the midnight oil last night as well. Tonight wasn't looking great either.

"Both phones are in a fireproof case in the box," she told him softly, "as well as a bunch of the most important paperwork we found. Maps."

Brown moved to the box and started removing items. He immediately called the techs for the phones. Within less than a minute, a team arrived and locked the box away. They would x-ray the box and do a dozen other tests before they even cracked it open, probably. It was like dealing with a hot potato in that they didn't know if the phones were rigged, so they treated them as if they were.

Hence, the private plane. As much as she would like to think it was to make their life easier, Amberly knew it wasn't. Less collateral damage if they did blow up.

"Frank filed several complaints with his immediate supervisors," Brown told them, "the most recent concerning me getting the job he thought he was supposed to have."

Amberly lifted her brows. "I didn't even realize he'd put in for it."

Brown nodded. "He did. And he was pretty pissed when

he didn't get it. He was even more pissed when his appeals were denied."

Cocking her head, Amberly thought about her recent dealings with Frank. He had bitched a lot, mostly about their new boss. Had her own perception of Brown been swayed by Frank's constant noise about him? Perhaps.

"So, with that being said," Devlin murmured, drawing the attention back to him, "maybe you should check your own house for his little presents."

Brown and Amberly turned to look at Devlin, then each other. Immediately, Brown reached for his phone, tapping in a number. Amberly realized he was talking to the director, getting permission to lock the complex down as they did a thorough search with the explosives crew.

Apparently, he got permission, because as soon as he hung up, the buildings went into lockdown. People were concerned, but not overly alarmed. They'd been through this drill many times because they realized they were one of the highest priority targets in the country.

It took them seven hours to find all of the Semtex charges Frank had planted, not just in their own buildings, but in the others in the complex as well. It took the crew two hours to go through her own building. So, they sat in the parking lot in an incident tent with reams of data going through intel until they were given the all clear.

It was a ridiculous scene.

Devlin stayed at her side for all of it, clarifying information as needed. They were both debriefed individually, which took hours, but it needed to be done.

The night was gone and morning was creeping over the horizon again by the time Brown told them they had a handle on things and to get out of there. "Temple, you have a significant amount of vacation time accumulated. Why don't you use some of it?"

Grinning, she nodded. "Will do. See you next week, boss."

"Kreed said he needs to get home," he continued, "so the plane is at your disposal. I got the Director's approval for that."

Amberly smiled, though her heart hurt at the reminder that they didn't live together anymore. "Thank you, Sir."

She started to turn away but Brown called her name and motioned her to the side. She was more than surprised when he stopped in front of her and leaned toward her a little. "I just want to thank you. My niece goes to Riverside. I made sure my brother took her out of school for a few days. They're running down the coast to see my parents for a while, just in case we missed something."

Amberly nodded. "Good. Probably smart, sir."

"You won't be recognized publicly for this, you know that, but the Agency knows exactly what you did for this country. And I'll be putting a personal letter in your file."

Emotion tightened her throat. "Thank you, Sir. Will it get me out of the cold case room and off your shit list?"

Brown looked at her, startled. "You were never on my shit list. I put you in there because I know the kind of person you are, and I knew you would find what others could not." He gave her a smile. "Have a good trip, Temple."

"Yes, sir," she said weakly.

They were driven back to the airport, their bedraggled bags over their shoulders. Requiem rested on the seat across from them.

Anxiety churned in her stomach, because they hadn't really talked about what was going to happen next. "Do you mind if I tag along with you? To check out your place?"

Devlin glanced at her in surprise. "I thought that was a given?"

She shifted and waffled a hand. "Not really. I mean, I don't want to impose. And you didn't really invite me."

Devlin snorted, catching her hand. "Amberly Temple, would you come home with me to Tennessee? I would love to have you."

Grinning, she leaned in for a kiss. "Yes, I will. Thank you for asking," she laughed.

21

D evlin couldn't have made the day any more perfect.

Amberly had woken him with a kiss, and they'd made love in the foggy light coming through his bedroom windows. They'd showered together, as they had every morning since she'd arrived. And she'd made them cinnamon pecan pancakes with bacon, his personal favorite. Now they sat on the front porch, watching the herd of deer he'd come to be cordial with cross his lower field.

Amberly had been entranced the first time she'd seen them. Hell, she'd been entranced for the better part of a week now, as he introduced her to his mountain home and his animals.

She and Tink had fallen in love with each other, though the pup was a little standoffish for a while. "She's jealous," Dev told her softly.

Amberly had laughed it off until she realized that Tink tried to intercede every time they hugged or kissed. And if they left the bedroom door open at night, well, that meant trouble. Dev had resorted to locking the dog in the laundry room every night, a situation Tink thoroughly disapproved of.

Everything else was perfect, though. Dev took Amberly fishing in the river behind the cabin, and took her horseback riding through the hills. Though she'd never owned a horse, Amberly had been enough places around the world that required horses for transportation that she was a competent rider.

Dev laughed as he chased her through the hills, and he loved seeing the relaxed, happy look on her face.

The 9-11 anniversary had come and gone, and there were no new bombings or attacks. They'd both scanned the news channels that day, and Amberly had given Brown a call. He had confirmed that no news was good news and told her to take another week off. She hadn't argued.

They were in the cabin making tomato soup and grilled cheeses one day when his phone buzzed.

You have a delivery.

He laughed, looking out the window. A truck was pulling in the drive, and a man stepped out. Tall and broad, he wore a ball cap to protect his face from the light rain. He started walking toward the cabin, and it took a minute for Dev to get moving. He recognized that slow walk...

Devlin opened the door. "Master Chief Garvey. I..."

"Hey, Dev," the big man grinned and wrapped him in a hug, pounding his back, then stepping away.

Dev was in shock. Since he hadn't heard anything from Charley, he'd assumed the deal had been bogus. He'd kind of been okay with it, though, because he'd been immersing himself in Amberly. She only had a little time, so he'd been entertaining her. The thought of his old team hadn't really even entered his mind.

"Come in, please," he said, stepping back.

Amberly was beside him, sizing up the other man. "Amberly, this is Master Chief Garvey. We always called him Gravy."

"Gravy is fine," he said, shaking Amberly's hand. "We've met, though it's been several years ago."

"I remember," she said cooly.

Dev remembered as well. It had been at his court martial. "Can I help you, Master Chief?"

Gravy looked around. "Mind if we sit down?"

Dev waved him to a furniture grouping in the living room and Gravy chose a chair, removing his hat as he sank down. He glanced around at the honey gold interior logs. "This is beautiful."

"I need to go turn the burners off," Amberly murmured, sensing the tension in the air. "Gravy, can I get you a drink?"

"Water would be fine, if it's not too much trouble."

Without a word, Amberly disappeared through the kitchen, and Dev was left with one of his former bosses. "Can I help you, Gravy?"

"I'm sorry to show up unannounced, but the bigwigs wanted this handled today. They're reinstating you, Moon Devil."

Devlin heard the words, but he wasn't as excited as he thought he'd be. At one point, he would have given anything to be back in his team, but he'd had three years to get used to being out.

Apparently, he'd been thinking for a while because Gravy leaned over to catch his attention. "Did you hear me, Dev? They want you back. We heard about what went on with Regent, and the CIA."

Ah, yes... the same issue that had been bothering him about being with Amberly. Now that he was proven to be in the right, and safe, not corrupt, they were willing to take him back. "I think I'm good, Gravy. If they want to modify my record to an honorable discharge and give me my retirement, I'll be happy with that. I'm not coming back to the teams."

Gravy blinked, surprised. "I thought for sure..."

"That I would want to go back to the team that didn't believe in me?" Dev finished for him. "That took the CIA's word over my own? No, thanks. There's a level of trust that a team needs to share."

"Dev," Gravy said, leaning forward, "you have to understand. They played us this recording and it sounded exactly like you."

Ah, yes, that doctored recording. He should have known. He relented a little, and tried to force a smile. "I understand, Gravy. But I won't be coming back. Thank you for asking." He stood up and moved toward the door, opening it. "If you'll let the brass know."

Gravy looked at him incredulously, then pushed to his feet. "I will." He stopped in front of Dev at the door. "I'm sorry, Dev. You're completely right. We should have had more faith in you. If you ever need us, please call us. We'd like a chance to make it up to you."

Reaching into his wallet, he retrieved a business card and handed it over. Dev took the card, but didn't look at it.

"Thank you."

And Gravy left.

Dev watched him go, feeling sad and frustrated.

"That was hard to listen to," Amberly whispered, "because I know I did the same thing."

He turned, finding her standing behind him, arms crossed over her stomach. "Yes, you did," he agreed simply. "And that hurts."

Tears filled her silver-gray eyes, and she rubbed them away with her fingers. "I'm sorry, Devlin. So very sorry."

Tears started to drip down her cheeks, and Dev had to move. Amberly wasn't a crier, no matter what. "It's okay, babe. I didn't love them the way I love you."

That made her cry harder. "Why would you tell me that? You're basically saying, if you love me you can hurt me."

"No," he said, chuckling softly. "I love you, and I realize that sometimes in relationships, one person gets hurt, but because they love the other person, they're willing to forgive and try again."

Her tears fell harder, and she sobbed, burrowing into his chest. They held each other for a long time, until Dev drew back to wipe her face. "I love you, Amberly Jade Temple. And I want you to know that I will always love you, no matter what."

"And I will you, too," she vowed. "I should have had more faith in you last time, but I didn't, and I'm truly sorry about that. I listened to what my head was screaming, when I should have been listening to what my heart was whispering."

He smiled down at her. "Thank you for that. And now I'm going to have some faith in you." Reaching into his pocket, he bent down on one knee, pulling out a stunning solitaire ring. "Amberly Jade Temple, I've loved you since the moment I met you. Would you be willing to marry this devil again?"

Laughing, she kneeled down in front of him. "Yes, happily. And here's my show of faith. Let's go to Gatlinburg and do it today."

Devlin laughed, taken off guard. "Seriously?"

Amberly nodded. "Completely. Let's go."

So, seven hours later, after pulling some serious strings, they were married in front of the Justice of the Peace in Sevierville, Tennessee.

Moon Devil couldn't have been happier.

EPILOGUE

Three weeks later, Devlin was still feeling a little salty with himself. Maybe he'd been too harsh with Gravy. If they had presented him with the same evidence about another teammate, it would have been hard to argue with.

Maybe he would call the guys once things settled down, and see about getting together...

If the CIA was good at anything, it was manipulating people and situations to suit the agency. They wanted him to take the fall for the hit, and he did. And even though they'd apologized, he had a feeling they would do it again if the situation arose.

Amberly had gone back to work a few days ago, and he was feeling her absence. They'd talked about what they were going to do going forward. Since Dev's business was small, he was thinking about restarting up there. He didn't want to be in the thick of government, but he would go up to be with her. Amberly had more time invested in the agency, and he knew she wanted to retire from there.

Hell, since they'd paid him his back pay he wasn't necessarily hurting for money. Maybe he'd see if Cliff wanted to buy the business or something. It was easy enough to start a new one. Once again, though, he would be leaving his friends behind.

They would just have to come down here for vacations. Perhaps they could keep the cabin, since they were going to be a two income family now...

Moon Devil.

He chuckled as he looked down at the text.

Hello, Charley. I'm not Moon Devil anymore. Didn't you hear? I'm officially out of the Navy, Honorable Discharge.

I did hear, and congratulations on your nuptials.

Thank you.

I never thanked you, officially, for everything you did. I had to go out of country suddenly, and I lost track of a few things.

No worries. You don't owe me any excuses.

There was a pause for a few minutes, then she came back. *I do, actually. And I made you a promise. If you check your bank account, you'll see I followed through.*

Dev sighed, sitting back against the truck seat. He'd come to work today, for the first time in weeks, and he was already missing Amberly. Nothing else really mattered. Regent was in his rear view mirror. *I don't feel like I should take money for taking him out. I kind of feel like I was doing my civic duty.*

Well, granted, you were, but the money was a small price to pay. Besides, diapers are expensive.

A deep, swelling pride swallowed him, and he grinned. *Heard about that too, huh? We just found out.*

I did. Congratulations, again. I wish you a safe, wonderful life, Devlin Kreed.

Thanks, Charley. You too! Don't call me again. Lol!

ALSO BY JM MADDEN

If you love dogs and would like to read about a concierge service helping military personnel out of difficult spots, check out:

Healing Home

Wicked Healing

Healing Hope

If you like a paranormal twist to your military, check out the Dogs of War! (If you love Christine Feehan's Ghost Walkers you should enjoy this series!)

Genesis-Free

Chaos

Destruction

Retribution

Catalyst

If you would like to read a Navy SEAL book with older characters, check out

SEAL Hard

Flat Line

If you would like to read about the 'combat modified' veterans of the **Lost and Found Investigative Service**, check out these books:

The Embattled Road (FREE prequel)

Duncan, John and Chad

Embattled Hearts-Book 1 (FREE)

John and Shannon

Embattled Minds-Book 2

Zeke and Ember

Embattled Home-Book 3

Chad and Lora

Embattled SEAL- Book 4

Harper and Cat

Embattled Ever After- Book 5

Duncan and Alex

Her Forever Hero- Grif

Grif and Kendall

SEAL's Lost Dream-Flynn

Flynn and Willow

SEAL's Christmas Dream

Flynn and Willow

Unbreakable SEAL- Max

Max and Lacey

Embattled Christmas

Reclaiming The SEAL

Gabe and Julie

If you'd like to connect with me on social media and keep updated on my releases, try these links:

✔www.jmmadden.com

✔My FB Like page- https://www.facebook.com/JMMadden58

✔Follow me on Twitter-- @authorjmmadden

✔Sign up for my Newsletter if you haven't already. You get 4 free books!

✔Follow me on Instagram- https://www. instagram.com/jm_madden_58/

✔The Lost and Found Series Discussion Group-https://www. facebook.com/groups/433871413415527

✔Tiktok- https://www.tiktok.com/@authorjmmadden

OR you can email me at authorjmmadden@gmail.com

ALSO-

If you love the book, **PLEASE** leave a review! We really do notice a difference when readers support us!

Thank you so much!

JM

Made in the USA
Las Vegas, NV
30 September 2021